Book
of
Iron

Book of Iron

ELIZABETH BEAR

Subterranean Press 2013

Subterranean Press
PO Box 190106
Burton, MI 48519

www.subterraneanpress.com

This is for The Jeff.

One

BIJOU BOLTED ALONE through the marble and lapis corridors of the Bey's palace like a messenger-boy fearing the back of his master's hand. The red-black springs of her curls bounced against her skull with each step. Her Northern shoes flapped in her hand; she ran barefoot, bare soles sure on checkerboard floors that had warmed already with the heat of the day. Behind her, something dry rattled as if in pursuit: Ambrosias, one of her artifices.

She didn't think Prince Salih would allow the photograph to be taken without her. Kaulas, however, would consider it teaching her a lesson.

Servants, ladies, and functionaries stepped aside to clear her path, drawing their robes against the walls. Whatever their rank, they knew it wisest to let a running Wizard pass.

They were dressed sensibly for Messaline's brutal summer. Bijou sweated already inside her black trousered suit, the height of fashion in clammy Vyšehrad but a ridiculous vanity in Messaline. But not a vanity Bijou was prepared to sacrifice today.

Kapikulu—scimitar-wielding door-slaves, sworn to the service of the martial god Vajhir—stood like pillars to either side of the corridor's end. Like pillars, that is, except for their coats the color of a sun-bleached sky. They also made no move to stop her, but in their case immobility was informed by confidence rather than caution. In fact, one reached out impassively and pushed open the pierced ivory door before Bijou hit it.

She let her steps slow so momentum carried her into the room beyond and onto its thick-laid carpets where three men waited.

Kaulas the Necromancer—handsome and hollow-cheeked and pale as mutton-fat, raw-boned in his height—stood against an inlaid cabinet, irritably smoking a thin brown cigarette. Each time his long rectangular hand lifted to his mouth, the bones of his wrist pulled free of his shirt-cuff and the sleeve of his suit coat. Bijou met his gaze and felt a chill like iron up her spine, a kind of hard and pleasant independence born in equal parts of her dislike for and her attraction to the man. It was easier not to like him. It kept her from making the mistake of too much vulnerability.

Beside him stood Prince Salih, the Bey's second son, who was clothed neck to sandals in a linen dishdasha of exquisite cut. In any other company, the prince might have seemed tall: next to Kaulas he was merely not dwarfed. He was a scimitar of a man, and the architecture of his face made him seem older than his years—or rather, timeless. Where Kaulas seemed tense, the prince gave off the relaxed well-being of a cat who had commandeered the best sunbeam. But Bijou knew that like that cat, he had claws: several firearms and a curved sword hung about his body in plain sight. More hung concealed in the flowing robes.

He gave Bijou a sleepy smile, crooking an arm to sweep her into the orbit of Kaulas and himself.

The third man bent behind the massive outline of a camera, fussing with fragile glass plates that must at all costs be protected from light. He was a pet of the prince's, and Bijou could not remember his name.

"Finally," Kaulas said, flicking the ash from his cigarette tip into a ceramic teacup rimmed at the edge with gold.

Bijou drew to a halt and drew herself up. The clattering behind her subsided as her familiar beast caught up, reaching the edge of the rug.

"I was busy," she said. "And I'm here now."

She clucked to Ambrosias without looking back at it. Ambrosias was an animate, bejeweled skeleton made in the design of an antediluvian centipede. At her summons, it swarmed up her body, the sharp tips of hundreds of feet catching at the fabric of her jacket. Finger-cymbals contained within its structure made a silvery shiver of sound as it draped itself around her neck, light catching on the rough-tumbled surfaces of jasper and agate set in sand-cast copper along its length.

Ambrosias was made of the vertebrae of horses and the rib bones of cats, articulated to a ferret skull. It stretched three canes in length. When Bijou turned, it twisted around her body like a spiral staircase. She composed herself in a posture that might not look too stiff, even though she must hold it for as long as it took the photograph to develop.

"There," she said. "I'm ready. Gentlemen?"

Ambrosias hated the flash. It clicked in distress, but held still because Bijou asked it to. Bijou was less irritated, but she too was glad when they finished and the prince sent the photographer on his way. She disentangled herself from Ambrosias, stretching the cricks of immobility from her spine. She let the bone centipede rattle to the floor like a chain of beads, and was about to suggest food when more running footsteps interrupted them.

These *were* the strides of a messenger, and one seemingly on urgent business. His feet slapped across stone to the carpets, where they were silenced. He ducked his head before Prince Salih, dropping to a knee.

"Salih Beyzade," he said. "There are foreign sorcerers to see you."

THE PRINCE'S REPUTATION meant a certain number of people with complicated problems sought his attention, sometimes unannounced. Because those problems were often the sort that no one but the prince and his Wizardly associates could assist with, he made himself considerably more accessible to the people than his father or older brother.

The people stood in enough awe of the prince—not to mention Bijou and Kaulas—that few of his supplicants abused the privilege. Most people considered it unhealthy to come to the attention of a Necromancer—even one who, under the prince's auspices, had devoted his tenure in Messaline to errantry and the noble deeds of an adventurer.

If foreigners had come in search of the prince, the odds were very good that something was very wrong.

Excellent. Bijou was in the mood for an adventure.

Stiffly, she permitted Kaulas to take her elbow and guide her, following the prince's long strides, to an audience chamber in the outer circle of the palace. The chamber was warded with sigils of lead and gold worked into walls and door, and glass spell-catchers hung in each narrow window, sparkling in the slanted light.

Two women and a man waited there, all three as pale of skin as Kaulas the Necromancer himself. Bijou felt the possessive pressure of his hand against the small of her back. She didn't think he tensed with recognition.

Foreigners, indeed. Foreign Wizards, if Bijou was any judge. And apparently the door guards had suspected the same, if they had ushered the three in here. Their stance told her more: they covered one another's backs and blind spots in much the same way that Bijou, Kaulas, and the prince watched out for each other. Adventurers, then—which explained what they were doing so far from home. While reaching Messaline from the North was no longer a matter of weeks or months of travel by ship or train, it still wasn't the sort of journey anyone would undertake lightly—and by their crumpled outfits and their cramped, stiff expressions, all three of these had been traveling for some time.

Bijou imagined she could smell the diesel and wind of a small aeroplane—like the one the prince maintained—still caught in their clothes and hair. She had experience with the cramped confines of the prince's craft: the ones available for charter were supposed to be much worse.

It was only natural that foreign adventurers would seek out the local talent. That was what Bijou would have done, if an investigation had led her to...wherever these came from. Having deduced the outline of their need, she turned her attention to the folk themselves.

The man had hair the color of red metal, curling long to his shoulders. Silver streaked the copper at the temples. He wore outlandish clothes, ill-suited to the desert heat: dark-colored pantaloons stuffed into soft brown boots, a patch-work cloak in every color swept off his shoulders. It must be some mark of estate, because Bijou could see the trans-lucent wet splotches on the shoulders of his shirt where it had rested. As he paced slowly beside the women, his stride hitched as if he had a nail in his sole. One shoe was spe-cially constructed to cushion a deformed foot.

He bowed low as the prince entered, flanked by Bijou and Kaulas, and the flourish of his courtesy left Bijou convinced he must be an entertainer or a courtier—if, truly, there were much difference between those two things.

Beside him stood a small woman with straight hair the color of wheat straw and the sand of the deep desert, arms crossed. She had lovely features made harsh by the strictness with which her hair was dressed back into a pony tail, and she wore unfashionable clothes suited for hard traveling, though they were not as archaic as those of the man. As he bowed, she frowned and jerked herself into an unpracticed curtsey, lowering her eyes a moment too late.

The third woman made no obeisance. She was tall, and skinny as a tentpole, which only reinforced the apparent youthfulness of her features. Dark hair coursed unfettered over her shoulders. Bijou remembered from somewhere that these northerners had two words for black, dividing it into the red-black of a black horse's hide and the blue-black of a black bird's wing. This would be the latter, the raven-black.

Her sharp-featured face wore an even sharper expression, and she was so clad as to remind Bijou of a magpie: a white, embroidered waistcoat or bodice buttoned over black blouse and scandalous black trousers not too dissimilar from Bijou's.

Bijou recognized the dark-haired woman as the leader, and not the sort who made obeisance to just anyone.

"Well met, Beyzade," she said to the prince, her words exotic and sharply accented with the rough vowels of Avalon. "Your reputation is wide. Your companions must be Bijou the Artificer and Kaulas the Necromancer, then? You are the famous Wizards of Messaline—defenders of the downtrodden, avengers of the despised?"

"You have us at a disadvantage," Kaulas said, glancing at the prince first to check his humor.

"Not for long, I'm certain," the woman said. "This is Riordan, a bard of my acquaintance, and the Wizard Salamander. And as for me—" she smiled, and stepped forward more fully into a fall of sun. Bijou caught the sparkle of sideways light through a peculiarly colored iris. The woman had one green eye, mossy and soft—and one the hard amber of a serpent's. *The evil eye.* "—I'm certain your confusion will remedy itself soon enough. Or is it possible that my reputation has not reached so far as Messaline?"

She wore a dagger in a brass-bound sheath at her hip like a tribeswoman or a barbarian, and she carried herself like a queen. That, the magpie wardrobe, and the mismatched eyes, were the clues Bijou needed to put a name to her—though in truth the young woman did not much resemble the descriptions of the storied Hag of Wolf Wood.

Well, it wouldn't be the first thing a storyteller had gotten wrong. Or oversold for drama.

"Maledysaunte," Bijou said, pronouncing it carefully in five syllables. *Mal-eh-thuh-saun-teh.* The Wizard with no Wizard's name, no *Doctor* and a pseudonym, as the Uthmans did it, nor cleverly suggestive noun, as was the tradition of Messaline. The Wizard who had trained herself, without benefit of ancient customs and institutions.

The young woman's face split with a wide, amused grin. "I guess it is rather obvious if you stop to think it through—"

"That's a fairy tale," Kaulas scoffed. "She'd be five hundred years old now, if she ever existed."

"Six hundred," Maledysaunte said. "And twenty-three. I know, I don't look a day over a hundred twenty. I'm a sport: my brother and I both were. Neither one of us aged much past maturity. I imagine he'd still be alive, too, if I hadn't killed him."

That was the root of the Hag's legend. She had been supposed to have sorcerously killed her half-brother, Aidan the Conqueror, when he would have made the tiny, sea-wracked Isle of Avalon into an empire to rival the ancient power of Danupati. That was all history, however. Most Messalines would not know that the Hag of Wolf Wood supposedly dwelt in Avalon still, secure in her cursed forest.

But most Messalines were not Wizards. And any given Wizard tended to know the history of magic, even magic of faraway lands and centuries.

"I see," said the prince. "And what brings the three of you to the City of Jackals? And, as importantly, to my friends and me?"

The Wizard called Salamander flipped her hair over her shoulder and spoke her first words. Her voice was quick and light, wry with self-mockery. "We're searching for the city of Ancient Erem," she said. "We understood this was the place to start looking. And as fellow adventurers, we would like your permission to proceed."

"You're fools," Kaulas said.

Bijou thrust her hands into her pockets, amused and irritated, as Prince Salih shook his head.

"Ancient Erem," the prince said, "is not the sort of place into which one trips lightly."

Maledysaunte paced quietly, three steps to and fro. Her arms remained folded across her bird-slight bosom. "But it is a place into which others have tripped, your highness. You and your friends, most famously." One of her hands unwound itself from the tight, defensive wrap to gesture widely, scooping them all in. "The tale of your exploits there, and how you ran the nefarious Dr. Assari to ground and brought him back in chains, has traveled far."

"Then so have the tales of Ancient Erem's dangers," Kaulas said.

Maledysaunte cocked her head. All three of the newcomers looked thin and drawn, expressions Bijou was used to seeing on the supplicants who came to seek the aid of Prince Salih's little band. But the black-haired woman had something in her expression beyond worry and tiredness: a sense of some deep knowledge that made even Bijou wish to recoil.

She said, "We know a little of them."

"You have a purpose beyond curiosity in going there, of course," Bijou said. Behind her, Ambrosias chimed lightly as a breeze passed through the chamber. Bijou looked to Kaulas for support.

He did not meet her eyes, but nodded nonetheless. "Your yarn—you should spin it."

"And see what we catch in its web?" Salamander laughed. She glanced at the bard: he waved her on. Bijou saw Maledysaunte bite her lip to silence herself. "I suppose we do. And if so, it is my tale to tell, though I will not tell it as prettily as Riordan would. We are in pursuit of an adventurer. One of the mystical sort. A Dr. Liebelos by name."

"How not," Prince Salih murmured, "when you are adventurers yourselves?"

Maledysaunte met his level look with a faint smile, a glance that said *How well we understand each other.*

"What has this man done to earn your wrath? And—more pertinently—mine?"

The Wizard Salamander sighed so deeply that her whole chest and shoulders rose and fell with it. "She is my mother," she said. "But that is not why we pursue her. Nor is wrath, exactly. We pursue her because she has a passion for antiquities. She's exercised it at several sites in Avalon, and as far east on the continent as the Mother River. With… predictable results."

Given his sallow pallor, it was easy to see Kaulas blanch. "And she's gone to Erem."

"You understand, then," Maledysaunte said coolly, "why it is we came to you."

With shaking hands, Kaulas lit another of his sticklike cigarettes. When it was glowing to his satisfaction, he said, "Ancient Erem…" and then paused for a puff or two, as if to steady himself. "Ancient Erem is cursed. Abandoned by the gods. It can only be entered by night, and there are other perils and conditions. Merely reading its script is said to blind the unlucky Wizard or scientist who attempts it. It is infested by ghuls and myrmecoleons, and it's only the ravages of the amphisbaenae that keep the latter in check."

"In Avalon," Maledysaunte said, "there are those who say the same of Wolf Wood, although those legends tend toward dragons and vipers. But I have never found it anything other than congenial."

Kaulas let the smoke coil about his face like the tendrils of one of the dragons the other necromancer named, but it was the prince who spoke: arch, amused. "And can the same be said by everyone else who has ventured there?"

Maledysaunte's thin lips pressed thinner, an ugly slash across her face. "They know what they're getting into."

"And now, so do you. Artifacts have been retrieved from that place…" Kaulas shrugged. "Does the good Doctor your mother carry casualty insurance?"

"Actually," Bijou said, "I am curious. The Wizard Liebelos. What is her specialty?"

From the press of Salamander's lips, Bijou knew that she and her friends had been intentionally withholding the information. Glances passed between them. Infinitesimally, Maledysaunte's chin dipped—the faintest of nods. So she was the leader of her little group, as Prince Salih was the leader of Bijou's.

"She's a precisian," Salamander said.

It was the rarest of magical specialties. As healers were rarer than necromancers, so the world gave birth to entropomancers galore—and only a very few of their opposites. Or complements, if you preferred—the Wizards whose art and science was that of perfected patterns and perfect numbers, of completed cycles and completed vows. Their magic was powerful and insinuating: it worked through mechanisms as subtle as the layout of rooms in a house or words in a promise. It could take years in reaching fruition, and those affected might never know.

The great precisians of history had propped up crumbling empires and founded colleges that endured a thousand years. They had a gift for making things permanent. Bijou suspected it was good there were so few of them. Otherwise the whole world might find itself trapped in unchanging amber, a fly unable to buzz.

If somebody with such an ability were to master the potent, corrupt powers of ancient Erem...Bijou would have liked to say the implications did not bear considering. But unfortunately, considering it was suddenly her job. The nausea and cold chills just came with the territory.

Should she obtain the powers of Erem, the foreign sorcerers' nemesis would wield all-too imaginable power.

"Irrevocable curses," Kaulas said, as if tasting it. "Enduring, impassable structures of death."

"You don't have to sound so happy about it." Bijou glanced at the prince for confirmation. His expression gave assent. "I think we can help you."

Two

MESSALINE WAS CALLED the City of Jackals, and jackals in quantity haunted its crooked streets. But Messaline had been built on the ruins of a previous city, a city rarely spoken of, as if to call its name might induce it to wake and shake the living city off its back. Messaline had inherited that city's epithet; the original City of Jackals was Erem.

And the Erem in whose bones Messaline stood was not even the first Erem. Out beside the erg, abandoned to the endless rippling dunes of the Mother Desert, there was another, even more ancient city—one not so much in ruins as simply abandoned where it stood, hewn from the living rock of a sandstone valley. No one was exactly certain why it had been left for the desert to reclaim, but visiting Ancient Erem was said to be perilous in the extreme. Legend held it to be not merely the haunt of ghosts, but the lair of monsters and of inhuman beasts that dined on human flesh. There were said to be curses there that lay in wait for the unwary, and insects that would burrow into a body and eat the brain from the inside out.

Prince Salih was not the sort to be put off easily by tales of ghuls and myrmecoleons, however. Once the Northerners argued their plan—and Bijou countenanced it—it seemed as if it took fire within him. He would not be content merely to extend them permission and as much of a safe-conduct as he was capable (which meant, in practice, however much the desert tribes might be willing to honor)—no, the prince himself would visit Erem. Again.

As if the first time had not been enough.

Which meant that his faithful friends and adventuring companions, the Wizards Bijou and Kaulas, must accompany him.

Bijou could not argue it: the precisian must be stopped. And surely six of them, half of whom were experienced in the horrors and pitfalls of ancient Erem, stood a better chance than three neophytes. It was the job; it was their duty. To the city and to the world.

Bijou sat before her vanity in the bedchamber she shared with Kaulas the Necromancer, oiling her skin and the roots of her hair in preparation for the desert's hungry dryness. She smoothed scented oil into her hands, polishing her dark flesh and pale palms to a shine. Behind her, she could hear Kaulas breathing. She watched his tall, spare shadow cross her mirror from side to side as he assembled his kit. They would set off at sunset, when there was light of twilight and then moon and stars to guide them, and they were well-shut of the killing heat of day.

"It's a fool's errand," Kaulas said. Although he, too, was a pale Northerner, his accent was very different from that of the sorceress Maledysaunte and her entourage. Kaulas was not from the western isles, but rather the rich land to the west of the great border city of Kyiv, near Vyšehrad. He'd once shown Bijou on the Bey's jeweled globe where his homeland lay. It didn't seem so far away, but Bijou knew it could take months or more of travel on foot to reach it. Even using ships and trains, it would be a matter of at least a week.

She'd imagined a land where everyone had the straight hair and fair skin of her lover. It would be a strange world. Where everyone looked like Kaulas, or Maledysaunte, or (even stranger) the almost-albino coloring of Salamander.

"I'd think," Bijou said, "that a return trip to a dead city where we nearly died ourselves last time…would be exactly the sort of thing to intrigue a necromancer."

He snorted. In the mirror, she saw him lift up a length of white cloth, smooth it carefully, and begin winding it about his neck and head so that it covered everything but his eyes.

"Do you think that's actually an immortal come to seek old Erem?" His voice echoed wistfulness.

Bijou's fingers curled in irritation. "Maledysaunte? I believe she's what she says she is. The Wizard Salamander is pretty, don't you think?"

"That type is at ten-a-penny in my homeland," he said.

Bijou noticed that it wasn't actually an answer.

"If she's immortal…" Kaulas settled a veil over his wrap, binding it in place with a red cotton band. Now faceless except for the squint of his pale eyes and the tanned skin of the bridge of his nose, he turned to regard her in the mirror.

The hostility in Bijou's expression must have warned him to drop it. She'd known for years that Kaulas was terrified of death: an ironic fear, she thought, for a necromancer. Or maybe one more justified for him than for most people. She didn't want to hear his conspiracy theories and self-pity about why Maledysaunte had managed to live forever, and he hadn't.

"We won't be in the sun," she said, replacing the stopper in her vial of oil. Ambrosias wound scratchily around her ankle, anxious not to be left behind.

"There's the morning to think of. We were lucky last time. You should prepare for daylight, in case we get trapped there over the day."

"As long as you're bringing plenty of water," she said. "I'll take some trinkets with me, I suppose."

She'd crossed the burning sands of the Mother Desert in sandaled feet once, but she'd been following the river then, down from its headwaters in the mountains where she was born. She'd been utterly unprepared and yet she'd survived. Erem, however…

Kaulas was right: it was stupid to let past luck make her careless now. She tucked some useful things into her pockets just in case—filters, a head-wrap, a veil.

She stood. She had changed her clothes to another man's suit, this one more rugged in its construction and of a lighter fabric: something suited for hours in the saddle and scrambling over rocks. Now she let Kaulas help her into a pale kaftan that would shield her somewhat from heat, wind, and sun. She tugged the sleeves down so only her fingertips protruded, then clucked Ambrosias into her arms. It swarmed up her like vines up a pillar in the rainy season.

"Pass me my sun hat," she said. "Just in case we're late coming back."

When he did, their fingers brushed with familiar electricity...and familiar loathing. She pulled her hand back, knowing all too well that if he was good for her, she wouldn't want him.

PRINCE SALIH AWAITED them in the courtyard, behind the wheel of a roadster no one else was permitted to drive. Maledysaunte already sat in the front passenger seat, the Wizard Salamander between her and the prince. In the second row, the red-haired bard had claimed the middle seat. He must have been wearing a sword at his belt, because now he held it—scabbarded and unslung—between his knees.

Kaulas split from Bijou, walking around the car to take the rear driver's side seat. Bijou settled into silky, squeaking glove-soft leather behind the Hag of Wolf Wood, pleased that Riordan had left her enough room for her hips without having to crowd in beside him. Long-legged Kaulas would be having a more awkward time on the opposite side. Bijou heaved the heavy door into place—it swung smoothly once she overcame its inertia—and made sure it latched. Even as it clicked, the roadster began rolling smoothly forward.

Normally, Prince Salih would not have gone out into the city unaccompanied by body guards—but he had long ago fought the metaphorical war with his father as to whether he'd be taking *kapikulu* adventuring. He had only won, Bijou thought, because he wasn't the heir.

The Bey's sons both loved automobiles. It was in their service that the roads of Messaline had come to be paved, and now Prince Salih's roadster purred velvety over cobbles laid flat and flush by master masons. They were carved of the same golden stone as so many of the old city's build-ings, but the blue twilight washed away all color, render-ing the walls and streets pale and ghosty. Messaline was coming to life with the sunset, the afternoon's high heat giving way to the relief of evening as a long, dusty, golden thread faded away against the western horizon. The top of the roadster was down: warm, arid wind made the coiled springs of Bijou's hair sway and brushed her cheeks like dry cloth.

The city stood on the banks of the river Dijlè, just above its confluence with the Idiqlè. Their reliable water in the vast desert was the reason trade cities had flourished and fallen and been rebuilt along their lengths for millennia. They crossed the river on one of Messaline's four bridges, an arched stone structure so narrow the roadster's wheels brushed the low walls at its edges. You could turn your head and look down directly into the silty, milky water.

It was fortunate, Bijou thought, that she'd ridden with Prince Salih in enough...varied...situations that she trusted his wheelmanship implicitly. If he'd been going to get her killed with his driving, it would have happened a long time since.

Bijou held her hat in her lap and tugged the caftan's collar up to cover her mouth and nose. She was paying for her vanity, while Kaulas looked at ease beneath his veils. The streets might be paved, but that didn't stop the dust from blowing over Messaline's walls.

The main road south, toward the deep desert, led them along the avenue of temples. Here the thoroughfare was divided, lined on both sides and along the median with date palms and pomegranates, shaded by argan, olive, sugar ash, and lime. Temples rose above the treetops, four large edifices dedicated to the principal gods of Messaline—Kaalha, Vajhir, Rakasha, Iashti—rivaled only by the palaces built to honor the nameless Scholar-God of the Uthmans, who was worshiped here in two or three denominations. Smaller cloisters, chapels, and shrines huddled between those of the major religions like chicks among hens.

These were not the only churches in Messaline. Nobody wanted to walk the width of a great city merely to worship.

But it was the highest concentration of monks and nuns in the known world, and Messaline's tourist industry was notably proud of the architecture.

As the roadster purred past the temple of mirror-masked Kaalha, Bijou realized that a sliver of crescent moon was following the setting sun into the west. Dawn and moonset were Kaalha's hours, and though Bijou had been raised to different gods in her youth in the two-sunned lands south of Aezin and the desert, she had adopted Kaalha as her patron here in Messaline. Under her breath, behind closed lips, she muttered a brief bene-diction. Kaulas noticed; she saw him leaning around Riordan to grin at her, only the crinkling of his eyes vis-ible above his dust mask.

She looked away, lips twitching with amusement. Kaulas too had converted to the religion of his adopted city—there was something to be said for honoring the gods who were observing the land where you happened to be—but he preferred the tiger-god of summer and high noon, red Rakasha. And after the traditions of his people, he kept his devotions private.

They motored towards the city gates, which stood open even at night in these times of peace. To reach them, the prince wended through mobs of pedestrians heading out for the night markets—some leading pack animals or push-ing barrows—and the inevitable bicycles, dogs, camels, and occasional man on horseback. Here and there, somebody cheered the prince and his entourage. Bijou had never been certain if that was just good politics, or if the people of

Messaline really did love the Bey's adventuresome second son. They'd be even more impressed, she thought, if they knew half of what he'd been up to.

Beyond the walls of Messaline lay hectares of rich farmland, hugging the riverbanks of the Dijlè and the Idiqlè. More date palms, vineyards, and the fallow fields of winter barley stretched to the horizon, shadowy and mysterious in the blue twilight—and then, as time passed, crisp and silver in the glow of the stars.

The roadster was equipped with headlamps. As the light faded from the sky, Prince Salih switched them on. Bijou regretted their dazzle: her eyes adapted to the brightness, so she could not see across the starlit fields. In the mountains of her birth and in the veldt they presided over like so many seated queens, stars were a rare sight, and total darkness rarer still. The single sun of Messaline, and the darkness of its nights, were precious to her.

Soon enough, they left behind the plantings for grazing land. Goats dozed on the rocky ground beside round-roofed cottages. The roadster's passengers engaged in idle conversation, Prince Salih explaining to Salamander and Maledysaunte what it was that they passed—which village grew olives, and which mined salt—and the names of the mountains in the distance. Riordan was curiously silent, a trait Bijou did not associate with entertainers. Kaulas pulled his veil down to smoke another cigarette.

The road turned away from the river and began to ascend, narrowing into a pass between high stony hills that were mountains only by courtesy. The suspension rattled over ruts and rocks. At the top of the rise, the prince let the automobile roll to a halt on the shoulder. He killed the headlights, and for a moment they sat silently in the desert chill.

It was full dark now, that scraped curl of moon long set, but the stars burned bright and close. It did not take Bijou's eyes long to adjust, and by the mutters from the front seat, Maledysaunte's adapted even faster. Necromancers could see in the dark.

Before them, a sea of sand stretched into the distance, heaves and swells robbed of color by the starlight. By day those slopes were red and tawny and streaked black with mica-dust along their lee surfaces. Now they might have been cast in beaten, tarnishing silver: the eternally breaking sand-waves of the seemingly endless erg. Bijou knew it didn't stretch forever—she'd crossed it once, as a girl who'd seen fewer than twenty harvests—but in the starlight it might as well have.

Riordan shifted on the seat beside her, his knee brushing Bijou's as he leaned forward between the seats. His flesh felt chill through the fabric of his trousers. She placed a hand on his shoulder to be sure, and felt his cool resilience. *Of course*, she thought. *If you were an immortal necromancer, you would want at least one companion who remembered all the years you remembered, as well.*

He smiled at her, the dead shoulder under her hand rising and falling apologetically.

She smiled back. Just because a man was dead was no reason to be rude.

Ambrosias, curled in a heap at her feet, rattled sleepily. "Right," Bijou said. She jumped up on the seat, sat on the door-edge, and swung her feet over. "No automobile beyond this point."

Heat still rose from the sun-baked earth, warming Bijou's feet in her boots even as the dry cold of the air raised goose flesh along her neck and shoulders. She turned to collect Ambrosias: it reared up atop the door and made a bridge to reach her. On the other side of the roadster, Kaulas was opening his door and stepping out with dignity. Riordan followed Bijou, even more nimble. He simply placed a hand on the door and vaulted over, swinging his legs high. Limp he might, but being dead obviously had not affected his agility.

"Shank's mare?" he asked without pleasure, surveying the slope down to the dunes. The breeze off the desert streaked hair across his face. He wiped it back with his left hand and seemed to test his stride against the sand.

Bijou shook her head, beads clicking in her hair. "We've come this way before." While Kaulas offered Salamander a hand out of the car, she set Ambrosias down beside the road and stretched up tall—or as tall as she could stretch—letting her rings sparkle in the starlight.

Then, with a glance at the prince—who paused in winching up the roadster's ragtop to nod—she lowered her arms and clapped her hands, glass bangles jangling like wind-chimes.

Maledysaunte shut the car door with a thud as Salamander stood clear. There was a pause, a long silence as the wind died away. Then Bijou heard the clop of hooves echoing along the pass, and a scrape like a stick across a grooved gourd. A few moments longer, and the starlight shone through the rib cages and illuminated the hide-hung skeletons of three horses, an ass, and a camel that made their way out of the rocks at roadside to stand before Bijou. They were all so old and weathered they smelled mostly of dusty leather and sun-drenched stone. One of the horses limped on a broken foreleg: that was the source of the rasping sound.

"You're a necromancer too," Maledysaunte said. "That makes three."

"I'm an artificer," Bijou said. "I don't bring the dead back to life, raise shades, or animate corpses. But bones have movement in them, or the memory of movement, and they are happy to move again."

Maledysaunte's gaze darted to the side as if something had drawn it. But just as Bijou was about to cry out a warning, Maledysaunte shook her head and pulled her gaze back to Bijou's face. Bijou, so appraised, felt an unaccustomed chill work through her on spiky spider-feet.

To dispel it, she gestured to Ambrosias. "I can work spells into an armature, and give personality and judgment. Autonomy of a sort. But those—"

Maledysaunte seemed to follow the gesture. "They move by your will. Not undead, just animated."

"More or less," Bijou said. "They'll carry us into Erem, anyway."

"Can't we walk?" asked Salamander, frowning dubiously at the camel.

"Only the dead," Kaulas said portentously, "may walk into dead Erem." He spoiled it with a laugh—a chuckle, really—at Salamander's stricken expression. "The camel is most comfortable."

The camel was most comfortable because the fat of its humps had saponified, so its riders need not rest their seats on its bare spine. But while Maledysaunte would probably find that intriguing, Salamander's night-shadowed expression indicated that she'd probably rather not know too many of the *fascinating* details about their mounts.

Prince Salih settled his rifle over one shoulder and circled the outside of the group, scanning the darkness beyond with a hunter's eye.

Riordan looked from one raddled corpse to the others. "I'll walk," he said. "It won't be a problem for me."

Kaulas made no comment—no reaction, in fact, at all. Prince Salih looked as if he might say something, but whatever he caught in the faces of those around him convinced him to school his tongue. "Well then," he said. "That simplifies matters."

The dead mounts knelt in the road. Bijou moved forward, throwing a leg over the ass, and pulled it upright with the power of her will. Although she was not tall, her feet nearly scraped the ground on either side. Desert-dry hide flaked crumbs away where her weight rubbed it against bone.

Maledysaunte reached out absently, as if brushing spiderwebs or an irritating insect away from her face, but there was nothing there. Kaulas helped Salamander on to the camel before climbing up behind her, steadying her with his hands at her waist.

Well, thought Bijou. Anger, jealousy, even irritation— they all seemed like too much work. She settled her sun hat on her head. It was easier than carrying it.

"Come on," she encouraged. "It's not far now."

Three

PRINCE SALIH WOULD have taken the broken-legged horse, out of chivalry or braggadocio, but Riordan's decision to trust his own twisted foot left the prince and Maledysaunte to the other two dead horses—mares, geldings, or stallions, it was beyond knowing now. When everybody except the bard was mounted—Bijou couldn't have said *settled*, not with the dubious look Salamander still wore—she turned to the prince. "Beyzade?"

"Lead on," he replied. "Try not to drop anybody down the cliff this time."

"This time," she snorted, turning the ass away. "As if I did before."

"This time," Kaulas answered from his perch high above. His knees dangled even with the prince's mount's wind-browned shoulder blade. "And every time after."

"We're coming back here?" Hiding her smile, Bijou shook her bunched kaftan over the ass's bony hips and urged it among the ragged rocks that hid a trailhead she and her partners had braved but once before. She had an electric torch in the pocket of her kaftan, but for now—until they made their way deeper into the canyons—the starlight sufficed. And a torch would give warning to their quarry, if Salamander's information was correct and she was to be located here. Ambrosias scrambled on ahead, cat-rib feet rattling along the stones and scratching in the sand. It would show her the trail. And she, in turn, would lead the party safely down.

It wasn't too long a descent. Ancient Erem had been well-defended by the mountains that surrounded it, but it had also been built to guard the pass where they had cached Prince Salih's roadster. Ancient Erem had also provided a first respite for weary travelers coming from the heart of the Southlands, in the ancient days when the Celadon Highway had flowed from far-away Song across the Steppes and the mountains and the desert, to meet other roads here. This trail had been a trade road then, and while it was no longer maintained, it was still adequately wide for a laden ass or camel.

Even one with starlight shining through the gaps in its ragged hide.

As the adventurers descended, the rock fell away on one side, leaving them wending down a narrow path with a cliff on the right and a sheer drop on the left. Right-handed defenders would have found it an advantage, even fighting uphill, against right-handed attackers whose weapons would have been fouled against that rough sandstone wall. The trail underfoot was sandy, too—it muffled the clopping of hooves and the scuffle of the camel's skeletal feet, but made uncertain footing for combat. Bijou was relieved that no threat reached them now.

At the bottom, there was no more starlight. She found her way down by following the shadow of pale sand against red rock and the ripple of motion that was Ambrosias. Relief bubbled up in her when the ass's bony hooves scattered grains across level earth. She paused in the dark, in the shadows of those towering cliffs, to see if her eyes would adjust further.

Kaulas could see in nearly pitch darkness. As Bijou turned back now, she saw the shine of his eyes like a cat's in the night. Maledysaunte's echoed the gleam. It was easy to discern which set of flatly shimmering discs belonged to which necromancer because one of her eyes reflected green, the other red.

Necromancers. Bijou wondered for a moment if, given the opportunity to dissect them, she'd find a *âyene cheshm*— the "mirror of the eye"—and, if so, if it grew there after they attained their Wizardry, or if they were born with shining eyes. It raised interesting questions about the nature of destiny and Wizardry, and how much freedom anyone could expect from the gods' intentions. What became of someone who was born to be a necromancer, but who felt drawn to some other branch of knowledge?

This is not the time for science, she told herself, knowing it for a lie. As far as she was concerned, thinking about Wizardry was a constant.

"This way," she called softly. Her voice reverberated back from every side.

She flicked her torch on, making sure the beam was pointed away from her companions and muffling it with a twist of cloth. To her dark-adapted eye, the light was sufficient to reveal the high stone walls all around them, the rough grit of looming sandstone—and the keyhole passage before.

The ass shuffled forward, peeling hooves scattering sand with each lurch. A chill breeze pushed at Bijou's face—not so cold or so strong as to bring tears to her eyes, but very slightly damp with moisture from the concealed oasis beyond.

"A cave?" Salamander asked, calling down quietly from the height of the camel's back.

"Just a passage," Bijou said. "Ancient Erem had excellent natural defenses." She paused. "Should we be sneaking?"

"Well…" Salamander paused judiciously. "…Dr. Liebelos is unlikely to try to kill me. But did you say something about monsters?"

"Oh, them," said Kaulas, still riding behind her. "They already know we're here."

Bijou ducked instinctively as the ass approached the passage. She would fit through—single-file—and so would those on horseback, though they might have to lie uncomfortably close to their mounts' bony spines. She'd have to send mounts back through for Salamander and Kaulas.

That was fine: once through the passage, she would be within Erem, and the prohibition that nothing living could enter would have been avoided by allowing the dead to bear them in.

She reached out with both hands to brush sandstone on either side, feeling dust and grit scrape her fingertips. Overhead, the walls did not come to a roof so much as meet in a peak: she could just have touched the highest point if she'd had stirrups to stand in. She still had to hunch her shoulders slightly, though, because of how the almond-shaped passage narrowed. The ass kicked grains of sand before and behind. The hoofbeats echoed faster now, the walls so close there was no sense of the sound bouncing back.

They came out of the tunnel into the great bowl-shaped amphitheatre of Erem. The ass stepped to one side and knelt, and Bijou—grateful to get the gouge of old bones out of her seat and thighs—stood. She was sore and stiffer than she'd realized. Too long out of the saddle. And too little saddle under her, for that matter.

Although a bare sliver of moon had set as they left Messaline, here in Erem three moons burned full and round in a dark mauve sky. One was pale, one red as rust, and the largest a dark shape so sooty it was visible more as a smudge, a shimmer of schiller effect, and a gap in the stars than as a heavenly body in its own right. Beyond the moons, that sky—more twilight than midnight—lay speck-led with a few handfuls of brilliant stars like those that showed through the gloaming, in Messaline.

By the time Bijou had shaken the desert-mummi-fied crumbs of leather from her trousers, Prince Salih, Maledysaunte, and Riordan were through the passage. Riordan walked slowly, tilting his head from side to side and then leaning it back to look up at the stars. As he cleared the passage, he glanced over at Bijou, his eyes vast and dark, his expression as placid as any statue's in the shrouded glow of her torch.

"Different stars," Riordan said. "Different sky."

"You thought this was a protectorate of Messaline." Bijou wondered what the sky of Avalon looked like. She'd read descriptions of its long evenings and skies as cobalt and indigo as the ocean—when the mist that normally shrouded them parted. She wondered what it would be like, a land so water-rich that people looked forward to sunny days rather than the rainy ones.

"Isn't it?"

"Of course," said the prince, shaking out his robes and stretching stiffly. "But Erem answers its own gods."

"And the gods of Messaline do not interfere?" asked Maledysaunte.

"I wonder what those gods of Erem are," Riordan said, as the two returning horse-corpses emerged from the tun-nel again, now bearing Salamander and Kaulas. Just inside the gate, Bijou allowed the desiccated bodies to lie down and be delivered of their burdens.

Maledysaunte's jaw worked as if she were withholding something. Whatever it had been, she replaced it with, "Pray we don't find out in person."

Bijou looked from the light to the sky, and flicked her torch off. It made little difference. She groped for her water-bottle and allowed herself a sparing sip. "The night was darker when we were here last."

"Perhaps it's just after sunset," Prince Salih volunteered.

"Just so long as it's not just before dawn," Bijou said.

Riordan looked at her curiously. But it was Maledysaunte who answered, "The midday suns in Erem kill."

She knew that, and Riordan didn't.

So what else was the foreign necromancer withholding from her team?

"Not just at midday," said the prince.

HAVING REGROUPED, THE party looked to Salamander. Salamander chewed her lip and rocked slightly on her heels, obviously stuck right on the edge of something. Uncomfortably, Bijou tried to find the words to help her, but empathy had never been one of Bijou's particular gifts.

She was half-surprised and half-not when Kaulas broke the uncomfortable silence to come to Salamander's rescue. But it was not as if Bijou had ever fooled herself that she loved him. Well, maybe once, long ago. But how many men were there for a woman who was a Wizard and an adventurer both?

"Well," Kaulas said. "Do you know where to find her?"

"Underground," said Salamander. "If I am any judge. But that leaves us a lot of options."

Kaulas laughed, though the joke hadn't been that funny. The Wizard Salamander regarded him curiously.

"Well," said Bijou, making a show of turning away. "I guess we start walking. Unless anyone wants to ride? No?"

She took her second long look at the disregarded city of Ancient Erem, cast out like a series of sand castles around the rim of the bowl-shaped valley. Sand castles cast in stone.

Erem had not been built so much as *mined*. In the moonlight, the starlight (seeming stronger now; that dusty mauve sky was fading to black violet) Bijou saw the empty doorways and windows of houses carved in terraces from the streaked stone. She knew the contrasting bands of dark and light were a red like dry blood and a white like exposed bone, for she had seen them in the first light of Erem's terrible dawn—before she and the others fled with their captive, the Alchemist Assari.

Now, it all looked gray and faintly blood-tinged in the light cast by the bloated red moon. Depth and distance fooled the eye in the twinned moon-shadows; one object bled into the next, and it was hard to tell what was real and what was illusion.

Beside those carven houses were larger buildings—or 'minings'—tall pillared faces presenting every appearance of having been constructed until you realized that at their edges, the walls merely blended into the stone behind. Bijou was minded of the blind faces of kittens pushing through the birth membrane, or—with their gaping doors like desperate mouths—perhaps the faces of the Bey's enemies as they were drowned in bags of silk.

She only thought of that, she told herself, because the scent of water hung so heavy on the air: a musty sharpness that promised life, relief, comfort despite the burning sands.

She knew it was a lie.

"Right," she called out. "If we should happen to come down by the oasis—don't drink the water here."

"Why not?" asked Salamander—genuine scientist's curiosity, Bijou judged. Not a challenge to her authority. Their eyes met, and the ghost-pale woman smiled at her.

Bijou felt a snap of warmth and camaraderie that erased any faint, lingering jealousy and replaced it with something else. Not a romantic interest—Bijou had ever been cursed by a preference for men—but a sense of welcome belonging. A lonely ache reminded her of just how long it had been since she'd had a friend of the heart, another woman to share secrets and sister-stories with.

"Cursed," Bijou answered, killing her torch since they had the moonlight now.

Salamander tipped her head from side to side, that strange bone-straight hair moving over her ears. "Good reason," she said.

She crouched down and dug her fingertips into the sand. Although Bijou was not familiar with the form the white Wizard's magic took, it was plain to anyone that it was magic she was working.

Something scurried across the sand to her, a pale body like a lump of butter, borne on eight fat legs. "Camel-spider," Bijou said, when Salamander raised her eyes questioningly.

"Nice and big," Salamander said. She drew a pin from her collar and pricked her thumb with it: the blood dripped, and Bijou was about to cry out a warning not to let it touch the sand when Salamander caught it neatly and smudged a dab on the spider's nose. If spiders could be said to have noses.

"She'll help us," Salamander said, standing. The spider raced away, vanishing over the rippled sand with a speed Bijou could hardly credit. "Follow her!"

But as she leaped forward, each footstep kicking a divot in the sand, Bijou heard something from the shadows of the cliffs that was not the rising wind or the rustle of sand on stone.

"Stop!" she called, and Salamander listened, skidding to a halt some ten canes ahead.

Prince Salih, beside her, must have heard it too. He lifted his head, turning, sniffing, eyes half-lidded in concentration.

"What was that?" the prince asked.

Bijou lifted her head to the wind in imitation of him, as if that could make *her* hear or smell better. "Something chittered."

A CHITTER—OR MAYBE the rattle of claws or something else hard, one upon another: it was hard to say definitively. But Bijou was pleased to note that Riordan and

Maledysaunte fell neatly into the back-to-back circle that she and her own partners established. The prince left his rifle slung across his back, but an automatic pistol appeared in each of his hands. Bijou knew those were not the only weapons concealed in the voluminous drape of his robe.

As they made their defensive circle, Salamander backed slowly towards them, her hands raised and empty. Bijou knew there were Sorcerers in the east who could throw light and fire, manipulating energy directly in a manner that no Wizard of Messaline had ever mastered. It was a different school of magic entirely, though one with its own roots in science. These northern barbarians were supposed to have derived their arts from the writings of medieval Messaline and Uthman Wizards—they even took their craft-names after the Messaline or Uthman fashions—but watching Salamander now, Bijou wondered.

"I see them," Maledysaunte whispered. "Dog-men. Along the cliff faces."

"Ghuls," said Kaulas. "They're more like jackals, actually."

"Oh. We don't have jackals where I come from."

Bijou risked a glance at the woman, a vanishing shape in the moonlight. "I'm going for Salamander. They're less likely to come after two."

Curtly, Maledysaunte nodded. Something gleamed darkly in her hand—a pistol Bijou had not known she was carrying.

"Whatever you do," Bijou said, in a louder voice, "don't bleed on the sand."

"Because it's cursed?" Riordan asked.

Prince Salih answered matter-of-factly. "Because it draws more monsters."

Riordan moved right, closing the gap as Bijou called Ambrosias to herself and stepped forward. "I guess it's a good thing we're monsters too."

At least he has a sense of humor about it. The dead horses and the ass were still slumped upon the sand behind them. Bijou reached out with her will and raised them, bringing them forward to flank her. It was harder to maintain the necessary concentration with her every sense straining into the darkness, but she did it. Ambrosias led her forward, its zills shimmering an incongruously cheerful sound within the cage of his jeweled skeleton.

The moons had not moved, but the shadows of the cliffs spread across the earth in inky blackness. Pooling. Reaching.

"Coming up behind you," Bijou said to Salamander. Prince Salih fanned out to her left, toward the nearer cliff, his scimitar snaking moonlight along the bezel like a bead of mercury. He'd have her flank. He always did.

Bijou said, "Have you a torch?"

Sand whisked in the gloom of the reaching shadows. They seemed to writhe forward. Bijou knew it was ghulish sorcery that made it so.

"Two," Salamander answered, without turning her head. "Should I use them?"

"If the ghuls come at you," Bijou answered. "The bright light will dazzle them. That shadow-weaving trick protects them from the suns, somewhat...but it can be pierced. Otherwise, don't use the torches. Who knows what they would attract?"

"Right," Salamander agreed, quite reasonably. "One nightmare at a time, then."

Her calm courage sent a pang of respect through Bijou. If she were to compete, not for Kaulas, but for Salamander's friendship—

But such a decision would tear the Beyzade's little party of adventurers apart as surely as a man quartered between horses. And what they did was important. They conquered dangers no one else could even approach.

One of the dead horses stalked up. Bijou was only a few canes distant from Salamander now. "Keep backing up," Bijou called. Another four steps, five, and they would be side by side.

"They're almost upon you," Kaulas called. Ambrosias reared up and rattled itself mightily, sending a warning shiver of sound across the sand.

Salamander gasped with effort, leaning forward in her determination, her open hands thrust wide. Through gritted teeth, she panted, "Too many of them. I can't...hold the shadows back."

As if a giant pressed against Salamander's palms, her elbows folded. She could fall back no further: with every step she gave, the shadows took two. They loomed close enough now that Bijou could see the gaunt shapes within, the yellow eyes gleaming with gathered moonlight. In the shadows, she couldn't make out individuals:

just a black silhouette of pricked ears and clawed hands, yearning.

Bijou made the dead horse whirl and kick, but it was slow and clumsy. In such things, she was a puppeteer at best, and these were not moves she had practiced.

"Let me," Kaulas called.

Normally, she'd hesitate to encourage him to raise up the shade of something so far decayed, but this was war. She released the wizardry with which she bound the horse-corpse, and felt Kaulas effortlessly pick up the threads before it could fall. Now the undead steed came alive, dry neck arching, hooves thumping the earth in a manner that could only be interpreted as a gesture of war. It threw up its head and shook out the sad, strawtick remnants of its mane. From its motion, Bijou imagined the fierce war-whistle of an angry stallion, but only the rattle of sinew and bone reached her ears.

The arrogant prance and kick of long, clean legs weathered down to brown bone broke her heart as no puppet-mastered corpse ever could.

The ghuls were not afraid of dead things. But even they must respect the flashing hooves of an angry horse—two, when the second corpse joined the first. A mare, Bijou thought, watching this one standing stolid and low-headed, sand blown from the jagged cavities where its nostrils once had flared. The shadows still stretched to encompass the defiant horses, though, and Bijou saw the undead mare twist her bony neck around and snap at a ghul-hand that clawed her shoulder.

Bijou reached out and grasped Salamander's shoulder, her fingers bunching cloth and sliding over the firm muscle beneath. Bijou saw Ambrosias's ferret-skulled head snap forward and rattle back, muzzle stained darker now, and wished—not for the last time—that she had thought to give it venom. As if Bijou's touch gave her strength, Salamander incrementally managed to straighten her arms again. Bijou leaned forward, heart hammering, willing the other woman strength.

The pressure did not push the shadows back. But it pushed Salamander away from them, into Bijou's arms. With that grip and the rear-guard of the horses and Ambrosias, Bijou managed to pull Salamander in retreat before the rising shadows. Shoes scuffling, sand sifting down over the tops of their boots, the women regained the circle of their allies.

As soon as Bijou and Salamander were clear, Ambrosias turned like a twisted ribbon and came back, legs wearing a rippled track in the sand. As Bijou released her grip on Salamander, Ambrosias swarmed up its mistress' leg and spine until it hooded her head, knocking her hat on its strings down her back and rearing up like a pharaoh's cobra crown.

The shadows lapped higher. Salamander, fumbling in her pocket, pulled out the torch. But before her thumb found the switch, Maledysaunte stepped into the gap in the circle, up to the edge of the ringing dark, and with her hands fisted at her sides cried out in a voice and a tongue that curled Bijou's soul like a dry leaf and made her hot blood as ash in her veins.

The words were ancient and oily, liquid and barbed. Bijou's stomach tightened against them. She could not get a breath. It was as if all life and light died within her, scraped from her body like nectar from a flower, leaving only the husk behind.

The shadows broke like waves on stone. Then they began to heap, climbing impossibly, as if piled against a wall of glass. They rose quickly as water running into a cistern when the gate is raised. Bijou saw Maledysaunte take a breath and square her shoulders, and more terrible words ripped from her like a torrent of wind.

The shadows before her were torn back, blown aside as if by an explosion. The corpse of the valiant mare, still snorting and kicking savagely as the shadows heaped over her, was blasted to splinters.

Bijou saw the ghuls clearly as their shrouds of darkness were ripped from them. The words did not seem to harm them, creatures of Ancient Erem that they were, only shredded them clean—but they seemed ridiculous in the naked moonlight. Nude, gaunt creatures that walked on a dog's misshapen paws, long ears cringing over the projecting bones of their shoulders, velvet-fuzzed grey skin mole-soft and defenseless. Their claws and teeth shone terrible, but their faces and bodies were frail. They minded Bijou of the big-eyed, hairless hounds some very rich men kept as evidence of their wealth: pitiful things that could bear neither sun nor cold without protection.

In the aftermath of the power of Maledysaunte's words, the ghuls straightened slowly, facing her, quiet with fear or surprise. What remained of the shadows they had commanded crazed, cracked, fell to dust and rolled back into the night. The red and ivory moons shone bright as lamps between stars that gleamed like the fires of a distant army, and all that light spilled down over a scene as still and orderly as an army of statues. Even the wind had died, and with it the ceaseless sifting of one sand grain over another.

"That was the language of Erem," Kaulas whispered. It carried in the silence. "How can you read it and see? How can you speak it and live?"

Maledysaunte turned her head and spat three rotten teeth upon the ground. The strands of her black hair that had blown across her face were bleached white and brittle. When she wiped her mouth, the back of her hand streaked dark and Bijou caught the rust-reek of clotted blood. Her lips, never lush, had withered like an old woman's, her youthful skin drawn up crêpey and puckered as if she were the toothless hag legend held her.

Four

MALEDYSAUNTE GLANCED AT Kaulas and touched her throat with two fingers, shaking her head lightly.

"She can't speak now," Riordan translated unnecessarily. "Not until her voice grows back."

"Grows...back?"

The bard spoke as mildly as butter. "She is an immortal, Wizard Kaulas. She will heal."

Bijou would have given anything to see the expression on Kaulas' face behind the veil. Just a glimpse of the thin band of nakedness revealing his eyes showed her awe and avarice.

He glanced quickly aside, as if he did not care to see her reading him. "It wasn't this bad last time," he said, voice still muffled by his veil.

"Indeed." Prince Salih pulled a fold of cloth across his face as if in unconscious imitation of the necromancer. "Would you say that something has their guard up?"

"I'd say," said Salamander. She reached to take Maledysaunte's arm. The necromancer shook her off and stepped forward, making a hooking gesture with her left hand. *Follow.*

She led them across the trampled sand, down into the center of Ancient Erem. The ghuls drew back before her. They lined the path, enormous eyes staring. Bijou found herself walking with the others, three abreast in two ranks. They measured their strides. The stamping, undead stallion followed them, shying and switching his tail as if the flies had not long ago had their way with him. Ambrosias lay flat and scrunched its forelegs into the cushion of Bijou's hair.

A line of cold froze her spine straight and stiff. She had made such a promenade before, down lines of hostile observers, at the beginning of the long walk that had brought her to Messaline as a girl.

She hoped this time the pejorative gazes would not be reinforced with hurled stones.

One ghul, gray and starveling as the others, pushed through to the front rank and prostrated itself before Maledysaunte. It hissed; it glibbered. Prince Salih moved forward, ready to intervene, but the ghul came no closer as Maledysaunte checked her step. Her lips formed words; no sound emerged. But its eyes watched the shapes her mouth made avidly, and it answered.

"It wants to know," said Kaulas, who spoke the language of ghuls, "if we seek the treasure-hunter. If we do, it says she went beyond the water."

"Do you trust a ghul?" Salamander said.

Kaulas and Maledysaunte, as one, shook their heads.

The ghul retreated, scuttling backwards on all fours. Bijou started forward again as if it had not accosted them. Out of the corner of her mouth, she spoke to Salamander and Maledysaunte as they came up beside her. "So, what say you tell us exactly what it was that Dr. Liebelos *did*, in Avalon? And what the results were?"

Maledysaunte just shook her head. No sound from her lips: not yet anyway. Bijou kept an ear on the footsteps of the men close behind them, but she wouldn't turn her head to see them. Instead she cleared her throat, a sound meant for encouragement. With some urging—it was heavy, being made of stone and metal and bone—Ambrosias slid back down Bijou's body and twined through the sand beside her.

From beyond Maledysaunte, the Wizard Salamander spoke reluctantly. "You've heard of the Glass Book of Erem?"

Despite herself, Bijou could not quite hold back the chuckle. "It figures prominently in the history of Messaline."

"There's another such text."

The moonlight was so bright that Bijou could see the color rise in Maledysaunte's white cheeks. It stood out in stark, discrete spots like the rouge on a porcelain doll from the outermost East. Her eyes flicked again, following some movement that Bijou could not. This time, Bijou understood it, and wondered how long one could endure, aware of things no one else could perceive, before it drove one mad.

"I see," Bijou said.

"The Iron Book of Erem. Also called the Black Book of Erem."

"Where is it?"

"Nowhere in the world, any more."

"Destroyed?"

"No," Salamander said.

From the set of Maledysaunte's chin, Bijou imagined she understood what the Hag of Wolf Wood was feeling. Bijou knew what exile felt like, the repudiation of one's family. But Maledysaunte's pride and distress were clues, and Bijou could not afford to pass those up, currently.

"I think," Bijou said, as they passed the last rank of ghuls, who turned to watch their backs retreating as they walked deeper into Ancient Erem, "that we've earned a few answers."

"When the Black Book has been read, it translates itself."

"Into...another language?"

The footsteps of the men grew ragged as they began to climb a slope to the lowest terrace of stone houses. The undead stallion's hooves slid in sand.

"Into the soul of whoever read it. It ceases to exist in the external world. In a very real sense, that reader *becomes* the book. And there it remains until that reader dies."

Bijou actually blinked, understanding running hot and habituating through her veins. The rush cleared her of the pall of sorrow and cobwebs Maledysaunte's incantation had left behind. She drew a deeper breath in reaction, thinking of rotten teeth and withered skin. "Which usually happens quite quickly, I imagine."

"I imagine," Salamander agreed.

"But Maledysaunte is immortal."

"She is."

Behind them, Kaulas cleared his throat. "That doesn't explain what brings your mother *here*, however."

Finally, a dim smile flickered across Salamander's face. Bijou caught it from the corner of her eye. "It's said that the one way to win the Book free of its...host...is to summon it back to the anvil where it was forged."

"Here in Erem," Kaulas said.

"Here in Erem."

Prince Salih asked, "What would that do to the host?"

Maledysaunte turned over her shoulder and smiled, a terrible grin that showed the gaps in her teeth and her blackened tongue.

"I see," said Salih.

"You could have warned us in advance," Kaulas said dryly. "Instead of spinning tales—"

"Spinning tales is what I do. Besides, would you have helped us then?" Riordan asked.

"We're heroes," Salih said.

Bijou shot Kaulas a sharp glare when he laughed.

They came to a funnel-shaped depression in the ground. Bijou turned left to skirt it.

"Watch out for that," said Prince Salih to the newcomers, interposing himself, one hand on the hilt of his scimitar.

Gently, he laid the other fingertips on Maledysaunte's arm to guide her away. She turned to him, eyes wide with surprise, and Bijou did not think it was offense. She was just shocked that anyone would touch her so informally, so without thought.

The flesh around her mouth was already plumping again.

"Myrmecoleon pit-trap," he explained gently. "If you fall in, you slide to the bottom—"

"Oh," she said, her voice rusty and worn—but present, and that was something. She swallowed wincingly. "That's not in the book."

Wordlessly, Bijou held out her water-bottle, and watched as the Hag of Wolf Wood took a painful sip.

"Maybe they're new," said the prince.

She rinsed the water around her mouth, swallowed, and said, "So. I suppose we're looking for the blacksmith's shop."

"Of course," the prince answered. "Where else would you keep your anvil?"

LOGIC LED THEM, along with the memories of Bijou and Prince Salih. An anvil would be on the ground floor; a forge would be well-vented. They decided rapidly that neither was likely to be located in the terraced houses stacked one tier on the next in the sandstone hills, turning instead to the largest excavations—the ones with pillared facades stretching up into the cliff-heights. But poking among them at random proved unhelpful, and every one of the adventurers was too aware of the lurking ghuls and of the remaining duration of the night wearing thin.

"There are a dozen," Riordan said. "Did your spider have better intelligence than we're likely to gain by choosing at random?"

"What about what the ghul said?" Riordan asked.

"A forge would be near water." Bijou volunteered the information as she realized it, having some experience with such things.

Salamander nodded. "I'm afraid my new friend was left behind in the stampede. But I got a sense of water from her, yes."

"Good," said the prince. "Water is this way."

"How do you know that?" Riordan asked—nevertheless following unhesitatingly.

They hadn't made it this far into the city last time. And there were no maps of Ancient Erem—none remaining, anyway, to Bijou's knowledge.

"Can't you smell it?" It was a testament to the prince's diplomatic skills that no trace of *helpless wetlanders* crossed his expression. Bijou was glad Kaulas went veiled, after all: there were none so scornful as those who had had to learn the hard way.

"Is that what that metal smell is?" Salamander asked.

"Yes," said Bijou.

"Then yes," she said. "I can."

The way tended downhill again, which was a good sign, and the night still darkened. Moons set, and soon they were walking only by starlight—but the starlight was enough. They avoided two more myrmecoleon dens, eventually coming upon a tall tongue of sandstone riddled with tunneled doorways. They might once have had rectangular corners, but over centuries the wind and sand had worn their edges smooth. The path downward led them around it, and here the drifted sand had blown back from an ancient road paved with cracked white slabs of stone.

As they walked, Bijou became aware of the brightening of the sky, even though the moons had long slid out of it. At one horizon—not where she thought East lay, in reference to Messaline—a dim glow appeared behind the canyon walls—a line of peach and gold and lavender tracing the top of the cliff face.

Salamander looked at her. "Should we be taking cover?"

"We'll have a little while no matter which sun it is," Bijou said. "I'd rather find your mother before she…"

…has time to kill your friend.

Salamander nodded.

Bijou said, "Pray one of the white suns rises first. If your gods are the amenable sort, pray that it's just the nightsun, and we're in a year where it rises far in advance of the others."

"How many suns are there?" Riordan said.

"Four," said Maledysaunte. "Three daysuns—the blue, the orange, and the white—and the nightsun, which is white also. The daysuns rise and set together; it is the blue one whose light is so feared. Sometimes the orange sun eclipses it, which is safer. A little. The nightsun is a wanderer. Like the moon of Messaline and the moon of Avalon, sometimes it shines alone in the dark, and sometimes it shines with its sisters. There is a pattern to its meanderings," she finished. "But it lasts a little over 1,864 years. And I'm not sure where we are within it. Once I get a look at the suns, I'll know better..."

The others had paused to stare, the dead stallion tossing his head in impatience as he checked his stride to avoid trampling Kaulas.

"Of course," the prince said to break the silence. "It's all in the book."

"The Book. The burning Book, the Black Book. The Book of flame. The Book, the Book, the Book." Her child-soft lips twisted apologetically. "My head is full of it. I could tell you their names in the Ancient Tongue—"

"Thank you," Salamander said hastily. "All the same."

Despite the pale light creeping up the sky, Bijou smiled. These foreign wizards had a sense of humor after all. Even if it involved a language whose every syllable was murder.

The adventurers rounded the end of that sandstone tongue and found themselves looking down into a deeper, narrower, and more shadowed canyon. Serried ranks of broken-topped pillars marched its width and length, showing that the whole thing had once been roofed in stone to form a hypostyle.

"They built in the valleys to stay out of the suns," Riordan said. "Gods, what a life."

"And what a death," Kaulas added. "They're all gone now, and what they built...." He shrugged.

They could not see a sun yet, but a pale brightness—
like the light of four moons—crept down one canyon wall:
the first light of the nightsun, Bijou hoped. The sky had not
paled much beyond that dusty mauve they'd seen on arriv-
ing, and she thought it was not yet bright enough to herald
the white daystar. Also the air still held the morning cool.

"I think we're in luck," said Prince Salih. "Or the gods
are with us."

"You trust them not to change their minds?"

"I think that ghul was trying to trick us," Riordan said.

Bijou shook her head. "Why should it, when it could
lead us to our deaths simply by telling the truth?"

She broke into a shuffling trot, her kaftan trailing in
the air behind. Running on dry sand was no joy: her calves
ached within strides and the sand that had sifted into her
boot gritted between the sock and her sole. But she con-
centrated on steadying her stride and her ankles as the others fell in. She could see the lakebed now, baked dry, with
the fragments of stone roof that had once protected it half-
embedded in the hardpan. It was difficult to judge how far
away objects lay in such a desert, with no haze to blur distant things, but Bijou guessed the hardpan ended no more
than an eighth of a league on—in the long, low arch of a
cavern behind it. In that deep shade, Bijou could just discern the glisten of water.

Limping heavily, Riordan was falling behind as they ran
until Kaulas stopped the dead horse and let him mount. The
bard might have been dubious before, but it wasn't because he
didn't know how to ride. He vaulted onto the stallion's back

with the same agility he'd shown exiting the roadster, and then he was in the lead at a rocking-chair canter. Clothing flapping, water bottles sloshing, the others raced after.

Bijou felt the air warming as she ran, the too-swift brightening of the rock wall—top to bottom—and then the sand at its foot as the nightsun slid over the edge of the cliff. It might have seemed no more than a star—it was a speck, surely no larger than a very bright planet against the fixéd heavens, and if it had any diameter its width was lost in its glare—but it was brighter than four full moons, easily bright enough to wash the velvet purple-black from the night and bleach it a heavy shade of lilac.

As the nightsun's rays caught Bijou she shaded her eyes reflexively, but in truth there was no need. The light was no more than a bright candle held over her shoulder, and far from enough to make her squint. What worried her was that the sky continued to brighten behind the nightsun's rising, incandescent lashings of molten gold and crimson staining half the shard of sky they could see from down in the canyon where they ran. She'd have pulled her hat up, but it wouldn't stay on her head while she ran.

"I hope you brought a parasol," Maledysaunte panted between steps. They were almost there. Less than a hundred canes distant, Riordan was already gentling the undead horse to a walk in safe shadow while those behind him pelted for safety.

"Smoked glass," Salamander gasped back.

"Polarizing filter," said Bijou, groping beneath her kaftan. The daysuns wouldn't kill her instantly, and the scientist in her cried out for a glimpse. To come so far, to stand under the last memory of the sky of a destroyed kingdom—what Wizard could resist?

They hadn't stayed for sunrise the last time they were here.

The sky overhead faded, and kept fading—through amethyst, orchid, lavender, to a horrible pallid shade, a white all dusty thistle-gray along the rim of the canyon. The heat fell down upon them, although the canyon was some protection: the cool air was trapped here and the savage heat only radiated in. Light burned down the canyon wall, brighter than any sun Bijou had ever seen, brighter by far than the twin suns of her childhood home.

Bijou thudded into the shade of the cavern with sweat washing tracks through the bitter dust that crusted her face, the corners of her mouth, the corners of her eyes.

"Kaalha be praised," she murmured, falling against the damp sandstone in the shadow of the cave. Behind her, the hardpan across which they had just run blazed with light, impossibly brilliant. Too bright to look upon. Too bright even to look toward.

The cloth across Kaulas's face was stuck wet to his skin. His breath made hissing sounds as he sucked air through it. And he was better off than Salamander and Maledysaunte, both of whom were crouched in the shade, hands on knees, gasping from the run.

"Polarizing filter?" said Prince Salih, wrinkling his brow.

Bijou fished it from her pocket. She pulled out a length of tight-woven beige cloth as well, draping it over her sunhat and her head as she edged around the shallow lake, back to the penumbra of the cavern's welcoming shadow. She pinched the folds together around the lens, a cut of crystal magicked to protect her eyes even—she hoped— from the wrath of such a sun as this.

She wasn't wasting time, she told herself. It would be a moment before the others had collected themselves enough to seek deeper in the cave.

Huddled in her makeshift blind, Bijou crept out into the light.

Even through the fabric, she could feel the heat instantly. It collected in the folds and scorched her fingers where she held the gather closed. But the suns—when she risked a quick glimpse—oh, the *suns*.

She had expected, perhaps, something like the suns of the veldt and the mountains—shining disks performing a stately courtship across the endless pale plane of the sky. But these were pinheads, negligible circles with an angular diameter no bigger than the sprocket-holes in a strip of silent-movie celluloid. The larger flamed a savage orange; the smaller burned actinic blue. It seemed as if only a diameter or two separated them, and a ceaseless tendril of flame curved across the space between to conjoin them. The fourth sun, as white and inoffensive as the nightsun, was a bright speck off to one side.

The heat was too much. Gasping in her shelter, Bijou ducked back inside the cave. How could that trifling thing drive her—already, after no more than a second or four—back into shelter, her skin prickling and sore where it had brushed the cloth? How could so much heat and brightness fall from so small—or so distant, more likely—a set of suns?

She groped for her water bottle and drank, swishing the water around inside her mouth so it would do the most good.

Back in safety, she folded cloth and lens and put them away. Her companions had gathered around Salamander, who crouched by the waterside. Bijou hoped they had remembered the warning not to drink. The dead stallion stood further down, sloshing water noisily with his skull as he tried to slake a thirst in flesh that no longer existed, but he was dead already: Bijou could not imagine the water would hold any terrors for him.

"That's something," she said, coming up to them. "Anyone else want to look?"

"Shhh," Kaulas said without rancor. "Salamander has found a guide for us."

Bijou looked down to see what the white Wizard held perched on her cocked forefinger. Orange as embers, and glowing softly in the shadows between a spatter of coal-black-dots...

"Of course," Bijou said. "It's a newt."

"An eft, actually." Salamander straightened up, licking her pinpricked finger again. Although it wasn't her place to judge another's magic, Bijou hoped there wasn't too much newt slime on it. "She came this way."

"Then by all means," said Prince Salih. "Lead us, my lady."

Five

AFTER THE FIRE of the outside, the cavern with its echoing, plashing water was a cool relief. Kaulas convinced the horse-skeleton to stand rearguard, and they arrayed themselves and continued downward, along the shore of the underground lake.

Now they needed the torches—even the necromancers, once they passed around a curve or two and out of sight of the entrance's reflected light. Bijou allowed the beam of hers to play out over the lake briefly, too entranced by curiosity to mind her own earlier cautions. The outer part of the cavern was raw and rough, wind-carved—but as they progressed backwards and it narrowed, they found themselves passing twisted filigrees of flowstone: stalactites, stalagmites, candelabras of stone that looked as if candles had melted and slumped down over them. The colors streaked and faded like the sandstone above, but this was something else—limestone, dissolved away and redeposited by millennia of water.

"We're under a sea," Bijou said suddenly, surprised. "A fossil sea. Limestone and sandstone."

"Imagine," said the prince. "This desert was water, once."

The chime of Ambrosias' zills halted abruptly. Bijou turned to track its jeweled gaze and saw something blunt-ended and swift coiling away among the twisted gardens of stone. Two bright spots in a light-banded black body caught the light of her torch before it vanished.

"Have a care," she said. "I just saw an amphisbaena." Then she realized that the guests might not have such things in their wet Northern lands. "A two-headed snake," she explained. "Extremely poisonous."

"And I," announced Prince Salih, from further down the lakeshore, "just found Dr. Liebelos's footprints. Or at least, the footprints of a woman with Northern boots, and not a ghul's bare feet and claws."

SALAMANDER AND THE prince led them through caverns and chambers for what seemed a long time. This was a natural cavern system, but Bijou could see the marks of the chisel here and there where it had been retouched to make passage easier. Still they walked hunched over or sometimes crawled on hands and knees, drenched in the cold, cursed water, struggling to keep the electric torches dry. The sand in their boots grew wet and wore the skin in the crevices of their feet raw. Bijou worried about infection—and about the curse.

The floors were uneven, the flow of the stream in many places dammed up behind what looked like constructed terraces. Bijou knew they were the result of mineralized water evaporating and leaving a precipitate behind, but that didn't change the wonder with which she observed them.

The caves were loud, resounding with running water and the footsteps of all of them. Confusing echoes fluttered all about. She wasn't sure half the time if she was hearing the footsteps of her quarry, or her own, or those of her party.

Half an hour in, Kaulas muttered, "Who puts a forge in the bowels of the earth?" The tallest, he was obliged to proceed in a painful hunched shuffle. They'd given him the last position.

"The eft is confident," Salamander said.

"And the footprints persist," the prince said, pointing one out where it was smudged into a muddy patch.

Riordan said, "It seems logical to me that we are seeking no ordinary anvil, but rather one with a special connection to some underworld god. Perhaps they only used it in ceremonies, and those were carried out here."

Bijou glanced at Maledysaunte. The necromancer's face was mostly a pale blur in the gloom, but Bijou was sure it betrayed concern. Whatever Maledysaunte knew—whatever her Black Book told her—she kept it to herself.

Bijou's eyes caught on a moving silhouette at the edge of the torchlight. "Halt!" she cried, her breath steaming in wet cold. Soaked clothes clung to her, and she shivered.

Everyone whirled, weapons ready.

But it wasn't Dr. Liebelos. The shadow that detached itself from among shadows was the outline of a naked man. His head was shaved, his face clean-shaven. In the torchlight his skin shone glossy dark, browner than Bijou's. Perhaps almost true-black—the red-black of a dark-hided horse, not the blue-black of Maledysaunte's hair or a raven's wing.

As he came closer, picking his way barefoot through the running water, the group of adventurers reflexively drew together. He didn't raise his hand to shield his eyes from the beams of the torches. Bijou found herself staring at his face, unnerved by something about its structure or expression. She took an involuntary step back when she realized what it was: even the whites of his eyes did not shine—because his eyes had no whites. They were simply inky pools from lid to lid, and within them, she imagined she could see a faint shimmer like the schiller albedo of the huge, sooty moon that had so recently set.

"Don't be afraid," the man said. "I mean you no harm. It's just been a long while since I saw your kind in the house of my ancestors."

There was something about him—a neutrality of presence. Bijou quested after it with her wizard's senses. He felt smooth and tepid to her mind. *Plastic.*

She was just figuring it out when Salamander said, "You're not alive."

"No," Bijou said. "He's a construct. An Artifice. Aren't you?"

"Aren't we all?" His tone was mild, amused. As sleek and room-temperature as the rest of him. Bijou noticed that even in the cave, it did not echo, though every other sound bounced eerily. "Whether we be made by gods or men is somewhat irrelevant."

He paused at a distance of two canes or so and spread his hands. The mud and water of the underground river did not cling to him, but slid smoothly off his...surface. You couldn't call something so poreless and frictionless a *skin*.

"What is your purpose?" Bijou asked.

"I am the guardian," he said.

"Are you here to bar our way?" He wasn't carrying any visible weapons, but that didn't mean he couldn't *be* one.

"I am an interpreter. I see to it that the will of the gods is recognized and understood."

Maledysaunte stepped forward, angling her body to move between Riordan and Prince Salih. When she stood at Bijou's shoulder, she squared herself and said, "What are you guardian of?"

The blackness of his eyes made it impossible to see where he was looking. "I know your voice," he said. "It was your voice that awakened me. You spoke words in the true tongue. You are the Book."

"I am," she said. "I seek the one who would destroy me. Will you let me pass?"

"I will," he said in his echoless voice. "And I will come with you, where you go."

Bijou put her hand on Maledysaunte's sleeve, drew the necromancer close so she could speak into her ear. "You don't trust that."

"You *can't* trust that," Kaulas interposed.

Prince Salih merely stood quietly, one hand upon the hilt of his scimitar, and watched them all with a gentle frown.

Maledysaunte drew back enough to smile at her. "I trust nothing," she said. "But he's in the Book."

Now THEY WERE seven, though the guardian's presence was not like a presence at all. A hush settled over them with his arrival, so even the splash of footsteps in cold water seemed curiously muffled. They crept in the light of Bijou's one dim torch until their eyes adapted—that is, the eyes that needed to adapt. For a long while, they did not speak; they only descended.

Salamander crept at the front with her newt and Prince Salih; Bijou walked just behind them.

The long silence was broken when Salamander said, in a whisper that nevertheless echoed, "You must think me an unnatural monster, who would hunt her own mother."

Bijou let the back of her hand—the one that didn't steady the torch—brush Salamander's arm—the one that was not bent up to support the newt. The white Wizard's words fell into Bijou's heart—a lump of old pain like a stone in a still pool. *And a mother who would not protect her own child? What kind of a monster is that?*

But the betrayals of Bijou's childhood were not Salamander's concern. Not yet, anyway. If this fragile connection between them ever blossomed into friendship, though—

Bijou began to think she might someday mention it.

"I think a courageous—a loyal—child protects her mother," she said, when she could get the words around the ache in her bosom. "That's why you're here, isn't it?"

"My mother," Salamander said. And, with a glance over her shoulder to Maledysaunte: "And my friend."

"Well then." Bijou nodded, as if that explained—and absolved—everything.

Perhaps it did.

Salamander turned her hand around and grasped Bijou's fingers. She didn't say *thank you*. It wasn't required.

Salamander squeezed. Bijou was still holding her hand when the river began to glow with a warm, amber light.

Salamander lurched forward without hesitation, dragging Bijou along with her for a couple of steps until they dropped hands. Salamander still held the hand with the newt balanced on it high and as steady as she could. "Run—"

Three steps, no more, with the feet of their allies pounding the sand and stone behind—and Bijou fetched up hard against a shimmering curtain of light that nevertheless felt hard and slick as a mountain of glass.

"Trap," she said. She turned her back to it to survey the rest of the group.

The amber light englobed them completely. It crept across the uneven floor underfoot; it gleamed among the stalactites overhead, giving them an appearance of melted wax limned by candlelight. Sourceless, shadow-less, it glowed steady and sure, even and bright, and did not flicker in the slightest. Its directionless shine flattened surfaces and washed out detail, making everything appear thin and papery.

"Amber," Kaulas said on Bijou's other side. "There's a symbolism—"

"Amber," Salamander agreed. "She's a precisian. What do you *think* it means?"

"Trapped in amber," Maledysaunte said. "Sealed away forevermore."

"Well," said Riordan dryly, "she wouldn't want to kill her daughter if she could avoid it."

The guardian, Bijou noticed, was not within their impromptu prison. Maledysaunte must have noticed too, because she cursed tiredly.

The remaining six fell in back-to-back, a defensive ring. Bijou's breath misted before her. "Cold," she said.

"The stasis bubble increases the effects of order," Salamander said. "Heat is entropy."

"She'll freeze us?" the prince asked.

"Only in time," Salamander said, avoiding glancing at Maledysaunte. "Long enough to finish her spellcasting."

"Right," said Prince Salih. "After all, 'she wouldn't want to kill her daughter.'"

Six

AFTER SEVERAL MINUTES, Bijou realized that—slowly, inexorably—the bubble of light was creeping in on them. She watched its curtain contract at about the rate of movement of the dawn's light crawling down a mountain. She couldn't hear the echoing trickle of water any more: all the sounds of the cavern were gone.

Ambrosias rattled at Bijou's ankles. Salamander tucked her small orange associate into her bosom for safe keeping.

"I know," she said. He reared up beside her, his ferret-skull head at the level of her shoulder. She thought if he could have, he would have hissed.

The cold raised the fine hairs on her arms, the nape of her neck. Her teeth ground together. Ice from the moist cave air rimed the rock and mud beneath her feet. When she shifted her weight, she heard ice cracking. Beside her, she could feel Salamander shaking. Only the bard seemed undiscomfited by the cold, and he had an excuse.

"Oh," said Maledysaunte from Bijou's back, "I think not."

She didn't speak those terrible words aloud again, for which Bijou was thankful. But Bijou turned anyway, feeling the presence of the Book within Maledysaunte as she raised up its aspect, and blistering heat rolled forth from her skin. Beside her, Prince Salih raised a sleeve to ward the side of his face. Bijou imagined she could smell his beard scorching. Riordan, on her other hand, seemed as unaffected by heat as cold.

The terrible heat baked Bijou's shoulder and the side of her face before she turned back, shielding her eyes. It was a destroying power, wild and terrible. Bijou felt it wrestling with the preserving chill of the amber light, leaving the rest of them a barely-habitable zone in the middle.

"Can't you mitigate that?" Kaulas asked.

"Sorry," said Maledysaunte, with no evidence of strain in her voice. "The Book was not written to *preserve* life."

The circle broke and reformed with Maledysaunte at the center, the rest ringing her within the band of light. Bijou squinted at the floor for several moments. Yes, the slow crawl of light had been arrested.

"Well," Bijou said. "That's doom staved off for a little while, at least. Now let's figure out how to break out of here."

"Punch through?" Prince Salih asked.

"What have you got?" said Salamander.

"Sword." Bijou heard the rustle of cloth as he shrugged. "Poignard. Bullets."

"No firing a gun inside the bubble," Riordan answered. "Did you bounce off that thing?"

"Ricochets," Prince Salih agreed. "You know, I'm not the one with the magic."

"No," said Maledysaunte. "Kaulas, I'm kind of busy. Do you think you can find a loose end in that and unweave it?"

"Fight order with chaos?" he said.

Her voice still showed no signs of strain. "Since we don't have a precisian of our own, fire with fire isn't exactly an option..."

"So we're all agreed that hitting it with swords won't work?" Riordan said. Maledysaunte's voice might show no strain, but that of the undead bard certainly did.

Bijou wondered what it was like, to be dead and still know fear. Could he feel pain? Did it matter? She didn't know enough about the traditions of the religions of Avalon to guess what Maledysaunte might be keeping him from— or if his own people would hold him just a soulless shell, the essential part gone on to a better place.

"Hit it and find out," Kaulas answered.

Riordan and Prince Salih must have a shared a glance, or some other moment of unspoken communication that Bijou missed, because they moved forward in unison to break the circle. Bijou saw the flash of swords in the amber light as they skinned their blades.

"You're rusting my sword, Maledysaunte," Riordan complained.

"Would you rather freeze?" she asked.

He hefted the northern broadsword—an ancient, crude-looking thing—and swung it over his head as the prince slashed at the amber barrier with his own ancestral scimitar.

It was as if two great bells rang on different notes. The reverberation seemed to start inside Bijou's head and shudder down to her toes. Rock dust shifted around them; the floor trembled against the soles of her feet.

The swords that Riordan and Prince Salih raised again blazed bright and true and razor-edged in the sourceless light, reflecting gleams this way and that.

"It sharpened my blade," said the prince. "Other than that, I don't think we hurt it." He sheathed the scimitar.

"Well," said Kaulas, "it's good to confirm the hypothesis. Let me try."

As the prince and the bard fell back, the necromancer stepped forward. Bijou watched his narrow form advance, caftan sweeping about the legs of the suit he wore beneath. She should feel something—Affection? Jealousy? Pride?— at this moment, but whatever the appropriate emotion was, it eluded her. Instead, mind racing for alternate solutions, she waited to see if Kaulas would succeed.

She imagined the ticking clock, the moment when— somewhere outside—Dr. Liebelos would complete her preparations and summon the Book, destroying Maledysaunte in the process. Would they freeze into stasis then, as the bubble of negentropy collapsed around them? Would Dr. Liebelos allow that to happen, despite her daughter's presence?

Would they even know it *had* happened until Dr. Liebelos let the bubble open? Could you die inside a stasis trap?

She didn't know, and under the fear and uncertainty that set her heart to beating raggedly and her palms to oozing sweat she realized she felt mostly the burning itch of curiosity. She was a Wizard, after all—a scientist at heart. She wanted to know the answers before she died.

Kaulas spread his hands wide as he approached the wall of the trap. Not a dramatic gesture: a practical one. Bijou could see the shimmers of heat collecting around his fingertips, stretching in streamers from his hands. There was no light, not yet. Just that warmth, and the infiltrating reach of it like bare roots spreading, seeking.

He brushed those dendritic extensions against the amber wall. It might have shuddered; the faintest of ripples might have spread through it. If they did, they left no trace in their wake.

But slowly, meticulously, Kaulas began insinuating the unweaving of his touch into the tight-spun order that held them in thrall. A dim glow traced their seeking, dull red like the afterimage of lightning strikes on the retina.

They did not so much flare as throb, pulsing in time with what Bijou imagined was the beat of Kaulas' heart. With each pulse they pushed in farther; with each dimming they receded. Not as much as they grew, however, and for a moment she dared to hope. She found herself leaning forward, fists clenched, rocking in time to that pulse as if urging a horse to a jump—*push, push, push now.*

Kaulas groaned, grunting with effort, leaning against the wall of the bubble, pushing his palms flat. Slowly, Bijou thought. Slowly, slowly, they began to sink through the amber light, wrapped in a protective glow like sullen embers.

The thunderous crack and the reek of ozone shocked her into a scream. Kaulas made no sound except the harsh whuff of expressed air as he was hurled back, arms blown wide.

Prince Salih stepped in and caught him.

It was one of the smoothest things Bijou had seen in a long partnership of smooth interventions. Kaulas might have been silent; the prince grunted thickly as the necromancer's weight struck him. But he was braced, and he only staggered a step backward before arresting Kaulas's ungainly flight. Bijou covered the distance in three running strides, relieved or furious to see Kaulas' eyes open blearily.

"Well." He raised his hands gingerly, still slumped back against the prince. They were raw, and looked sore. "I've identified one of its defenses."

"I'll say you have," Bijou said, swallowing irritation and amusement. The damned man had an uncanny ability to make her feel two contradictory emotions simultaneously. She took him by the elbow and steadied him to his feet as the prince pushed. "Now what?"

Nobody spoke, though guilty glances were traded. Guilty, Bijou thought, because everybody felt a responsibility to get them out of this—and nobody had any productive ideas towards that destination.

Or perhaps she was projecting.

HAVING ACHIEVED A stalemate, they waited and paced and thought. Bijou found it necessary to rotate often, in order to even out her temperature exposure between the furnace of Maledysaunte and the icebox of the stasis bubble. It was that—the tension between hot and cold, chaos and order, that let the first threads of the idea drift through her mind. There was something there—but if she pursued it, she knew, she was as likely to knock it away as pull it closer. Like butterflies, ideas were best ignored and left to alight when they would.

So she paced, too, and stared at her toes, and felt the anxious closeness of her comrades at arms for some time before the tickle turned into an inspiration.

"Maledysaunte," she said.

The necromancer looked up, pulled from her own brown study. "Bijou."

"You said the guardian is in the Book. There's no indication that this could be his doing?"

"None whatsoever."

"And no reason for him to be helping Dr. Liebelos?"

"I imagine," said Maledysaunte, "that the Book's destruction is the last thing he'd desire. It can't make any mischief if it's not out in the world, after all."

"And he's a creature of entropy himself."

"Yes."

Bijou nodded. "And if he wants the Book out in the world, he's going to want *you* out in the world, isn't he?"

Maledysaunte stood taller, her dark hair breaking over her shoulders. They were attracting the attention of the others. They gathered now, leaning forward, interested.

"We don't need to disassemble the stasis bubble," Kaulas said. "Just punch a hole in it, and then he can help."

"That was my thought," Bijou said. "Can you and Maledysaunte do it by working together?"

There was a pause as the two necromancers eyed one another.

"I'd have to stop holding the bubble open," Maledysaunte said eventually, slowly. "If it didn't work, I don't know if I'd be able to re-establish control."

Bijou glanced at Prince Salih.

"Do it," he said. "I have no desire to find out if I can die of thirst inside a stasis trap."

It had just been waiting someone's determined word to stir them all into action. Maledysaunte took a deep breath, closed her eyes to concentrate, and unwove her spell. Bijou watched as she opened them again, breathed deeply, and stretched her neck until it cracked.

The returning cold broke over Bijou like a wave.

"Right then," Maledysaunte said, and took Kaulas' raw-fleshed hand in her own.

It was much as before, except this time Maledysaunte and Kaulas each placed one hand on the wall—his right, her left—and leaned into it. And instead of a lightning-craze pattern of dull red threads, what grew before them was a spiral that turned into itself over and over again, writhing, twisting. Bijou tried to watch, but even to a Wizard's eye, the arcane twisting was nauseating.

She felt the change of air pressure when they broke through, though—and the sparkle of new energy joining them. The guardian must have been waiting for just such an opportunity.

That black hand—utterly black, as if light fell into it, like a shape cut out of the universe—lunged from the gap they had made, and reached toward Maledysaunte and Kaulas. They grabbed his fingers with their joined hands, and there was an abrupt pop—not so much a sound as the shift of air pressure against the drums of her ears.

The stasis bubble unraveled like a snagged sweater, leaving them standing in the chill of the cavern surrounded by the echo of the water running down.

"How long?" Maledysaunte asked the guardian as he stepped back, lowering his hand.

"Thirteen seconds," he said.

Bijou felt her eyebrows climb, but said nothing. Of course, time had slowed inside the bubble. Of course it had.

Seven

THEY BEGAN TO smell burning soon after. A dull glow crept around a curve ahead, limning the crooked edge of the stone. Bijou turned off the torch and they made their way forward on tiptoes, each one testing each step before committing his or her weight. Another few cramped strides brought her to the corner.

Mouse-soft, Bijou leaned around the edge and peered up a limestone dam almost as tall as she was to a great cavern that flickered with light and heat. The warmth of wet air made her realize suddenly how cold she was and had been. Skin that had long since stopped stinging and settled into the corrugations of gooseflesh burned anew.

The stream broke over the dam to her left, trickling down the surface in a series of rivulets in yellow and white limestone channels. Beyond that—beyond the limestone wall she faced—another small underground lake stretched to a stony bank beyond. It was from that bank that the light and the smells of burning emanated.

A woman bent over a great stone block, a stalagmite whose top had been sliced away to make a flat surface. A great black anvil was set upon it. Bijou the Artificer owned anvils of every shape and size, from a silver-working rig you could balance on the palm of your hand to a monster four men couldn't lift. This was the largest she had seen.

The light and heat came from a forge nearby. As Bijou watched, aware of the rest of her group slinking up behind her, the woman—pale-skinned, stripped to the waist except for a leather apron, her long light hair twisted into a straggling knot at the nape of her neck—moved easily between one and the other, stirring coals and checking heat levels. Bijou noticed that there was no bellows and no smoke. *A magical fire.*

"The Forge Unquenchable," Maledysaunte whispered.

Bijou gave her a sideways look and whispered back, "It's in the book?"

Maledysaunte nodded. "It is where the Book was forged."

Their voices should not have carried across the lake, but perhaps Bijou should have thought about whispering galleys and the acoustics of caves. Because the woman—Dr. Liebelos, of course—stood up from her forge with her fists in her back and stretched tiredly. Sweat gleamed on her face as she said, "Is that you, Wove? I've been expecting you."

"Wove?" Kaulas asked.

But even as he spoke, Salamander moved forward. She set her eft down at the edge of the water and turned right, to clamber up the jumbled boulders that slumped there. They made a kind of awkward ramp or stair, and Salamander scrambled up it.

"Her cradle-name," Maledysaunte said, already moving to follow. "Let's not wait for an invitation."

Riordan required an assist to get up the bank, but still they made it as a group, in seconds. Salamander had paused at the top, hanging back until they could join her. Now the seven moved forward as one, six following Salamander across a narrow stone bridge. Bijou was braced, Ambrosias clattering along beside her. If she were defending that forge, she would strike when her enemies were bottlenecked on the cane-width span.

But Liebelos just watched them come, her hands at her sides, until they reached the far bank and fanned out, three on each side of Salamander.

Bijou noticed that Maledysaunte kept the black-man construct close beside her. His presence—or lack thereof—still discomfited Bijou deeply. But Maledysaunte was right—bringing him along had been the best solution. What else could they have done? Try to fight him, when they were in a hurry, he'd done nothing to provoke them, and they knew nothing of his powers? Leave him behind, and have him following out of sight?

Keep your friends close, and your enemies closer, she told herself. It was good advice: and for now, the enemy was Dr. Liebelos.

Except Liebelos was tossing her round-headed hammer casually to the rock beside the anvil and wiping the sweat from her palms onto her leather apron as she came forward. "Darling," she said, extending her hands to Salamander. "I knew you'd come around. And you've brought your friend..."

She didn't acknowledge Riordan at all, and her eye only skipped appraisingly over Bijou, Kaulas, and Prince Salih. She did give the guardian a considering glance, though.

"Mom," Salamander said, "I've come to talk you out of this madness."

"It's not madness," Dr. Liebelos insisted. "This is necessary. I'm a precisian, Wove. A scholar of order. Trust me when I tell you that it is a ticking bomb to have the Book present in the world in a form as capable and enduring as Maledysaunte's. It is a pattern that will remake all our world in its image, with the Hag of Wolf Wood its possessed and terrible demon-queen."

Bijou was close enough to Prince Salih to see his eyebrows rise in the light of the smithy. "A precisian complains of an excess of order?"

"Just because I am a scholar of order," Liebelos said, "does not mean I am always its partisan."

With a shrug of dismissal, she turned back to the forge and anvil. From here, Bijou could see that what she had taken for coals were no such thing. Pellets of stone filled the

Forge Unquenchable, as Maledysaunte had called it, glowing white-hot. The air above them shimmered with heat as Dr. Liebelos moved toward the forge.

She lifted a set of tongs from a rack and reached into the coals with them. As if miming, she drew the tongs back, holding nothing in the tines.

She laid the nothing on the anvil. Left-handed, she took her hammer up. She raised it high and struck a ringing blow, hammering air against forged steel. In the flickering red light of those coals that weren't, Bijou saw something begin to shimmer into existence between anvil and hammer, in the grip of the tongs.

Eight

PRINCE SALIH GLANCED at Maledysaunte. "What's to stop us from just walking up and grabbing her?"

"There's magical energy accumulating with every blow of that hammer," she said. Her pale face drew in over the bones beneath it, collapsing as if each strike against the anvil pulled blood and strength from her. "I can contain it. I will contain it. But the longer you wait...."

Salamander stepped forward. "Mom," she said.

She paused at the edge of the hammer's swing. Liebelos didn't hesitate.

"*Mom!*" Salamander yelled, more forcefully.

The hammer came down ever harder. Bijou could see the ropes of Liebelos's muscles moving under sweat-slick skin. The sweat flew from her face, dripped from her nosetip to sizzle on the anvil. The blows reverberated within the enclosed chamber, dizzyingly loud, like the pound of a heart if you stood inside it. The anvil itself grew hot, hotter with every blow. The shimmering shape upon it resolved, clearer and clearer, like an image on a photographic plate emerging under the developer.

It was, of course, a book. A folio volume, as tall as the reach of Bijou's arm, bound in hammered iron, the cover hinged more like a door than like the spine of a book.

Bijou saw Salamander nerve herself. She saw the moment when the white Wizard made the decision to step forward, under the hammer-blow. She saw Maledysaunte sagging, dropping to one knee in the limestone-laced mud of the cave floor, her head drooping as if her neck were a wilting flower's stem.

And she saw Prince Salih step in as Liebelos drew the hammer back to her heels for one more tremendous swing, and catch the haft in his right hand.

"No more," he said.

Liebelos tugged. The hammer would not come free. She released the hammer haft and whirled on the prince. "You must let me continue," she said. "The fate of worlds hangs in the balance."

"A life hangs in the balance," Prince Salih said. He lifted the hammer one-handed, reversed it, and let the head rest on the floor. Upon the anvil before him, the book began to fade.

Maledysaunte lifted her head. She gasped in a breath, harsh and rattling.

"No," said the guardian, in his voice without echoes. "This is not what happens now."

He reached out, a gesture as effortless as the flow of oil across water, and grasped Salih's right forearm. His hand closed. Bijou heard the sharp wet snap of a bone breaking.

Another man might have gone to his knees. Salih released the hammer-haft; it stayed steady for a long moment before falling sideways. Before it touched the mud, Salih had a pistol in his left hand, pressed against the guardian's abdomen below the ribs.

He fired.

Pain as if someone had clapped a spiked palm to each of Bijou's ears lanced through her head.

The guardian's flesh jumped away from the impact as if the bullet had been a stone thrown into still water. The bullet thudded against the far cavern wall. Limestone powdered in the impact. The sound was lost in the thunder still ringing in Bijou's ears. Then it collapsed back as seamlessly, leaving him whole and untouched.

He looked at Prince Salih as if terribly disappointed in him. The prince, dazed by his own gunshot or the pain of his broken arm, shook his head.

Carelessly, the guardian extended his arm and threw Prince Salih against the far wall. Bijou did not see him strike. She was already moving forward, Ambrosias at her side.

The guardian fixed her with a stare from the bottomless, lusterless black pools of his eyes. "Don't."

Bijou froze. She couldn't hold his gaze; she twisted her face aside to see Maledysaunte climbing to her feet, the dead bard supporting her. Salamander crouched down, clutching her knees as if trying to make herself impossibly tiny and so go unnoticed. Kaulas stood over her, the picture of a protector, his kaftan flaring wide in the cavern's constant breeze.

Bijou couldn't hear his voice, but she wouldn't even had needed to read his lips to know what words they were shaping. "I *said* not to trust him."

"We didn't," Bijou snapped back, her words muffled and dull inside her own head.

The guardian's words were not lost in the crashing thunder ringing through Bijou's ears. They sounded just as flat as ever, and just as pellucidly clear.

"Dr. Liebelos," he said, "pray pick up your hammer again."

Belatedly, it occurred to Bijou to wonder how it was that he spoke their language, if he was a creature of ancient Erem.

Bijou could not spare a glance for Prince Salih. She hoped he was alive. In her peripheral vision, she saw Maledysaunte struggling to stand, propped by Riordan on one side. Kaulas moved forward to assist her, coincidentally screening Salamander from the guardian's view. Behind him, Salamander—still hunched piteously—dug her fingers into the sand.

The ringing was dying down, though not fading away completely. Through it, Bijou heard Salamander saying over and over, "Don't hurt my mother. Don't harm my mother."

Dr. Liebelos approached cautiously, crouching and reaching out to hook the haft of the hammer with her fingertips and slide it toward her. Mud and grit stained her trousers to the knee. Her fingers blanched white where they pressed the haft. She stood, dragging it toward her, and turned back to the anvil.

She swung the hammer high.

"Guardian!" Bijou cried, stepping toward him just as the hammer crashed down.

His head, only, swiveled, the rest of his body as motionless as a praying insect's. "Do not interfere," he said.

Bijou stopped beyond his reach. She sidled one step, another. "What Dr. Liebelos said about saving the world. You have to get the book out of Maledysaunte, is that right?"

He simply regarded her. Gasping, Dr. Liebelos drew the hammer back for another effort.

"Because it will corrupt her?"

The corners of his mouth twitched.

She sidled another step. Now his back was to Salamander and the ragged Maledysaunte, who seemed now to choke on every breath. She had gone to her knees again. She clutched her throat, and with the second hammer blow fell to her side, legs kicking as if she were suffering a seizure. Perhaps she was, but Riordan and Kaulas were beside her to guide her down.

"You don't care about saving the world," Bijou said. Of course there was no point in explaining his own objectives to him—but she needed to keep his attention, and Prince Salih had already demonstrated that a direct assault was not the way to do it. And even constructs loved to talk about themselves...

The hammer rang again. Bijou didn't steal a look. She knew the book—or the Book—would be taking shape on the anvil. It didn't matter.

What mattered was keeping the guardian's attention.

She said, "I think I understand you better than that. You don't want the book out of Maledysaunte because it will make her some kind of witch-queen. You want it out of her because it *won't*. Isn't that the truth? She's strong enough to live with it. And as long as it's in her, it's not destroying anything else."

She was guessing, and his expressionless mask of a face gave her no advice as to whether she was guessing correctly. The hammer fell again; this time the thud was duller, as if something interposed between it and the anvil.

Maledysaunte arched against the mud, gagging on a scream. Kaulas leaned above her, holding her shoulders down. Her feet kicked brutally, leaving long gouges where the bootheels scraped.

"O Child," said the Guardian. "You are blind."

"Fine," Bijou said, irritation rendering her incautious. "So tell us what you *do* want. Did it ever occur to you to ask for help?"

It certainly never occurred to me, a little voice mocked.

"The book must be destroyed," he said. "That is the only way I can be free of this existence."

"You must have had centuries to destroy it," Bijou shot back. "Just getting around to it now?"

"I cannot wield the hammer," he said.

"And if it can't be destroyed?" Riordan said, rising up and leaving Maledysaunte to Kaulas.

Oh, Kaalha, she prayed. *Don't let him make the guardian turn around.* If he caught sight of Salamander...

But Riordan came around a circle to confront the guardian at her side. "Then better to have it out wreaking havoc in the world than in safe containment, aye? In the witch's head, it can sit safe forever. Where's its mischief, in hands like hers?"

Whatever the guardian might have replied, it was lost in Salamander's scream as she suddenly stood up and hurled her arms over her head. It wasn't any kind of magic, just sheer stagecraft.

The guardian turned in his footprints, a hand coming up as if he meant to reach out and grab Salamander by the throat.

Something pale and swift struck from the water's edge, hurling its long length through the mud to sink needle-fine fangs in the guardian's calf. Bijou had a brief, confused image of hissing and a flickering tongue, a muscular writhing and then a shape like a bent bow as the amphisbaena whipped its other head out of the mud and plunged the second set of fangs into his neck.

He flailed, a hand coming up to grab at the snake's midsection, but it was already gone—whipping itself end over end to somersault into the darkness like a hurled stick. Bijou had a moment to observe the thin trickles of black ichor that oozed from the bites—something that had not happened when the bullet passed through him—before he turned away to face Salamander over Maledysaunte's convulsing body and Kaulas's back.

Kaulas, Bijou realized, wasn't just holding Maledysaunte down. His hands were inside her waistcoat, rummaging.

Bijou might not be an expert in assessing the emotional states of demigods, but she knew Kaulas. He was looking for a talisman, whatever might hold the secret to Maledysaunte's immortality.

"Oh, for fuck's sake," Bijou spat. "In the middle of a battle? *Kaulas!*"

She shouted that last as a warning, but the guardian wasn't looking at the necromancers. His gaze was fixed on Salamander. One hand was raised to his throat; ichor slipped between his fingers and trickled down his arm, dripping from the point of his elbow to the floor.

The hammer rang again. Bijou thought the blows were falling farther apart. Dr. Liebelos was tiring. Prince Salih was lying somewhere in the cavern, possibly broken and bleeding. But he'd proven that without the guardian, they could physically intervene with Dr. Liebelos.

"Riordan," she said to the bard beside her. "Get the hammer."

He asked no questions, just stumbling away up the slight incline to the anvil. The mud dragged at his bad foot.

Across the cavern, Salamander shouted, "Natural weapons!"

Of course. The snake's teeth hurt him. Bullets did not. Fists and feet, then—

Bijou leaned back and kicked the guardian right in the small of the back. Behind her, sounds of struggle rose as the hammering ceased. Salamander bent down, scooped up a rock, and hurled it at the guardian.

Maledysaunte's hands came up and grasped Kaulas's fumbling wrists. "Off me, you whoreson sorcerer!"

He didn't move fast enough to suit her. She twisted against him, using her hips to throw him off—and directly into the path of the guardian as he leaped toward Salamander. Maledysaunte dragged herself up, a terrible figure in her mud-soaked clothing, lurching toward the anvil.

"Can't beat the guardian," she snarled, falling in the mud up the hill. "Got to remove his reason for fighting."

Whatever his other failings, Kaulas reacted to his unexpected impact with the guardian by latching on—and lashing out with feet and fists. Bijou fully expected him to go flying in a moment, as the prince had.

"Mother!" Salamander cried, racing after Maledysaunte. But Maledysaunte was already at the top of the incline, where Riordan had Dr. Liebelos by the wrist. She twisted to get away from him.

Natural weapons, thought Bijou, as Ambrosias reared up out of the muck and sank its pincers into the guardian's neck, below the base of the skull.

The shearing bite would have paralyzed a human; on the guardian, it only succeeded in connecting because his arms were encumbered by Kaulas. The guardian hurled the necromancer off into the mud, where he crumpled.

Prince Salih came limping out of the darkness, one arm dangling limply, his face a demon's mask of blood and mud. With his good hand, he leveled a pistol at the guardian.

The guardian reached over his head to grab the articulated centipede. Ambrosias dangled from his fist, rattling like a string of beads.

"No!" Bijou shouted, crouching to scoop up a rock as big as her fist. She wound her arm back—

The guardian stopped. His fingers opened. He dropped the bone and jewel centipede in the thrashed and slimy soil.

Bijou followed the line of her gaze.

Maledysaunte and Riordan stood beside the empty anvil, the hammer slack in Maledysaunte's hand. Dr. Liebelos was a huddle at their feet. Salamander had stopped halfway up the hill, frozen in horror, hands spread wide as if she could arrest the moment.

"It's over," Maledysaunte said to the guardian. "Go back from whence you sprang."

She let the hammer drop from her hand.

Nine

RIORDAN CARRIED DR. Liebelos's body from the cave. Prince Salih leaned on Bijou, but he walked—and Kaulas and Salamander walked also, supporting one another. Maledysaunte went first, alone.

Bijou thought it was so she would not have to look at anyone.

"What about the blood?" Salamander asked, the only words anyone spoke as they came up out of the belly of the earth, their way lit by many electric torches now that there were no concerns about conserving the batteries.

"It summons myrmecoleons," Kaulas answered. "Maybe if we're lucky, we were too far underground for them to notice."

"And if not?"

"Another fight," Prince Salih said tiredly.

No one spoke of Kaulas' attempt to rob Maledysaunte during the battle. No one spoke of Maledysaunte's killing of Dr. Liebelos. For one terrible moment, Bijou had been afraid that Kaulas would offer to bring her back for Salamander—but apparently even he could read that much in the wind, and he kept silent.

Leaving the cave seemed to take three times as long as coming in, even though they simply followed their own footsteps back.

When they came out by the water, the dead stallion awaited them. Over his protests, Prince Salih was installed as the animal's rider, as he was the most-wounded. Bijou knew it was the right choice when he slumped with exhaustion on its back, even his iron will insufficient to the task of keeping him erect.

Night had come again in the depths, or at least twilight. But against it, Bijou could see the hunched, scuttling shapes of myrmecoleons lured from their dens by the smell of something wounded. They had humped, chitinous ant-bodies and fierce-toothed cat-heads wreathed in shaggy, sand-matted manes.

"Well," Kaulas said. "At least it's not a manticore."

"I've got it," Salamander answered. Using Kaulas as a prop, she crouched low and scratched her fingertips across the earth at lakeside. Whatever she muttered, Bijou did not make out the words.

But the myrmecoleons withdrew, and made a ragged honor guard for them as they left.

"Nice work," Bijou said.

Salamander stared through her, but didn't shake off Bijou's hand when Bijou put it on her arm, ignoring Kaulas as if he were no more than a convenient prop.

Bijou gave her a squeeze. She felt Salamander lean back.

Somehow, she didn't think the white Wizard would be going back to Avalon with the necromancer who had killed her mother.

They trudged past the myrmecoleons and began the hasty journey back to the trail in, racing the killer light of the suns.

"Kaulas," Maledysaunte called from the front of the line.

He went up. Salamander leaned more heavily on Bijou, now that they walked alone. Maledysaunte didn't look at Kaulas as he walked beside her, and made no effort to lower her voice when she spoke. Bijou heard them clearly.

"There is no secret," Maledysaunte said. "I was born this way. Perhaps my half-brother and I were the bastards of a god, as has been rumored. But if so, that god has never chosen to identify himself to me. And he has been content all these centuries to let the old King take credit for his begetting. Do you understand?"

"Yes," Kaulas said. He had the dignity not to offer a spurious apology.

"Next time," Maledysaunte said, "I will kill you."

He walked beside her in silence for a little, until it became obvious that she had no more to say. Then he fell back to walk with Bijou and Salamander again. Bijou let him take over: as for herself, she joined Maledysaunte with a few quick strides. Ambrosias's cymbals chimed as he scurried to keep up.

"The Book makes me see things," Maledysaunte said without preamble. "Usually, I manage not to look."

Something burned by overhead, a cold streak of greenish light. A meteor, a shooting star. After a moment it was followed by another.

"You'll be fine," Bijou said. She heard the unspoken request for reassurance under the plain statement of fact. "You're strong."

Maledysaunte grunted. As they made their way toward the waiting skeletons of ass and camel, the dusty violet sky overhead was lanced with meteor after meteor, tearing down through the heavens to light the world below with fire.

LATER—AFTER THE DAMAGE to the prince's upholstery (he managed to drive, but Bijou had to sit beside him and shift); and after Kaulas abandoned his animate skeleton among the rocks; and after baths and food and sleep—later, Salamander told Maledysaunte and Riordan she would not be returning home with them. Maledysaunte nodded understanding. "If you ever need me," she said.

"If you ever need me," Salamander replied.

Both, Bijou thought, knew the other had no intention of asking.

Maledysaunte and the bard took their leave of the others, including Prince Salih with his dishdasha draped awkwardly over the sling and cast confining his arm. Now they walked away, and Salamander stayed behind until the messenger had led them out of sight.

Then, without a word, Salamander turned and left as well, going deeper into the palace as Maledysaunte and Riordan had walked out. Prince Salih walked beside her as if they had planned it in advance. Bijou imagined they hadn't.

When they were out of earshot, she had something she planned to say. But Kaulas beat her to it.

"I wanted to make you jealous," he said. "Do you know what you're like? It's like trying to hold a cloud, Bijou. Like clutching at mercury. Nothing ever touched you. Nothing ever pierces you."

Bijou watched Salamander's receding back, stiffly erect as she walked beside the prince. He would see her settled, Bijou knew. When he had accomplished that task would be time enough to trouble him for new rooms of her own.

"And you wanted to be the thing that put holes in me? How romantic you are."

He said, "I did."

She said, "You didn't succeed."

She meant more than the jealousy. But Maledysaunte and her dead man were gone, already vanished down the corridor to the prince's waiting car. She couldn't send a significant glance after them.

He glanced at her, sideways and down. "Not this time, my love."

Ten

IJOU HAD EXPECTED silence from Salamander, at least for a little while. She had a sense that the other woman would prefer to nurse her grief alone, and up to a certain point she would respect that. Bijou the Artificer was not the sort to make other people's choices for them, or assume that she knew what was best for anyone. Even, she thought bitterly, her own self.

Because if she did, she realized now, she never would have gotten involved with Kaulas. Her own loneliness notwithstanding, she didn't have it in her heart to be the thing he needed. And it had been unfair of her to allow him to delude himself for as long as she had.

Unfair, and unkind.

Knowledge was not always courage, though, and she didn't find it in herself to move her things out of their shared room. She knew he was giving her space, hoping she would circle back to him. And she—she didn't have the strength to sever what she was coming to think of a dead limb.

When she sought Salamander out, it was for her own solace, not that of the white Wizard.

THE PRINCE HAD made Salamander comfortable. Her rooms were airy and shady both, on the garden level and protected from the Messaline sun by a broad verandah. Bijou wondered if she'd ever be able to think of this sun as fierce again, having known the suns of Erem.

The rooms opened onto the courtyard with a series of louvered doors. These stood open, and Bijou was not surprised to find a heavy-headed snake patterned in a dark and pale knotwork of sand colors, with beige dots decorating each joining of the darker weavings, resting in the dappled shade. She stepped around it carefully and paused in the doorway, calling out.

Salamander sat at her desk, which she'd turned to face the bank of open doors. Not a woman you'd care to creep up behind, Bijou judged.

The viper's tongue flickered, but it did not uncoil.

"Bijou." Salamander spoke calmly. She weighted the scroll she had been studying to hold her place, then rose. "Careful. There's a desert cobra under the foot stool."

"And a saw-scaled viper by the door." Bijou had more respect for the viper than the cobra, frankly: Messaline's breed of cobra was quick and shy, a glossy black snake that wanted little trouble with anyone. The vipers, though—a grown man bitten by one would die bleeding from every orifice, convulsing horribly and moaning with the pain. It was considered kinder to put a bullet in a man's head than allow him to pass that way.

"I knew you'd seen her," Salamander said. "Wine? Unless you'd rather have tea? Will you sit?"

"Wine would be lovely." Bijou gestured to the low divan. "Any other crawlies?"

"The scorpions are all under the bed," Salamander said. "There are some spiders around somewhere, but I've asked them not to bite. I assume you'll try not to step on them in return?"

The corners of the room were already draped with intricate swags of web. And not all of Messaline's spiders were spinners: most lurked and jumped.

"We'll call it even, then," Bijou said. She settled herself while Salamander brought wine on a tray. She—or someone—had set up an ingenious arrangement of mirrors that brought cold light into the corners of the room. Salamander moved around, fussing with the focus, and came and sat beside Bijou as Bijou poured.

They turned toward one another, knee to knee, and Bijou touched her cup to Salamander's. The wine was cool from the cellar, sweet and tangy with the flavors of green berries and spice. The vapors made her lightheaded as witchcraft.

Bijou sipped twice before she spoke again. The wine might not give her strength, but at least it could buy her time.

"I'm sorry about your mother's death," she said, hearing the words as alien. They each had meaning, surely—I and am and sorry, about and your and mother. And death.

Each one had a definition, a usage. Together they formed a sentence. It wasn't the words, really, was it? It was the sentiment. Mothers. So much need. So much love. So much opportunity for misery.

But Salamander paused, the wine raised to her lips, and set it back down untasted. "It wasn't your fault," she said. "She made her choices a long time ago."

"Still," Bijou said. "Still."

"Yes," said Salamander. "Still."

A silence followed. Bijou heard the wind soughing through the leaves of the date palms and pomegranates in the courtyard. The heady scents of a thousand flowers rose from the cultivated beds.

Salamander pushed her cup aside with her fingertips and stood. "Come on. Let's go for a walk."

The courtyard garden was big enough for strolling, and deserted—except for the *kapikulu* who dotted it like statuary. They walked along paved paths between the bowering leaves, the tangle of branches. It reminded Bijou of the jungles of the South, beyond the Mother Desert—but here it took a rich man's will to create what nature had decreed would not exist.

Golden tamarins—a monkey imported from halfway around the world—scampered in the tree limbs. They were smaller than a cat and far more agile. Their long tails flashed behind them like banners as they leaped from branch to branch. Behind the flowers and the shrubberies, Bijou could make out the roofline and the fluted golden pillars of the Bey's palace defining the space.

Salamander spoke in a low voice, encouraging Bijou, too, to hush her tones. "I had nowhere to go."

"Back to Avalon?" Bijou asked.

Salamander shrugged. "Maledysaunte gave me the excuse. But I've been needing something different. To get away from the mistakes of the past, I suppose."

That pang of identity that Bijou had felt far too often in Salamander's presence pierced her again. It was unfamiliar, that familiarity.

"I'm sorry for how it came about," Bijou said. "But I am glad you're here."

Salamander gave her a smile. "Maledysaunte and Riordan have each other: after a few hundred years, I suppose you grow accustomed to thinking of outsiders as temporary."

Bijou nodded. "I don't envy her."

"Or him?"

Bijou shrugged. She'd been thinking of the bard as Maledysaunte's familiar, she realized. As something like Ambrosias: an artifact of wizardry. But he'd had an identity before he died, hadn't he? He'd been a person. And that person was still intact.

So what was it? A transformation? A state change? When did he lose his own identity?

Ambrosias, she realized uncomfortably, had had an identity before she created it, too. Many identities. Cats and a ferret, although they'd all been long dead before she salvaged their bones. Did stones have minds? Did metal? She knew that across the sea and the salt desert to the East there were stones that lived, and moved, and ate other stones.

That way lay madness, she thought, and the lives of the religious ascetics who would not wear shoes, because they were walking on the face of the Earth, and who starved themselves rather than eat a once-living thing.

"He has something he believes in," Bijou said. It was inadequate, but it was what she had.

Salamander nodded. "The Hag of Wolf Wood." Then she sighed. "It's hard when one is alone in the world."

Thinking of Kaulas and of what passed for a love affair in her life, Bijou opened her mouth for the obvious comment. *Everyone is alone. We come into this world alone, and so do we leave it.* Then she realized it was a lie—a facile, comforting lie disguised as bitter cynicism. Did the bitterness make it seem like medicine and truth, when in fact it was a lie?

Because no one was alone. Every action, every choice— it vibrated like a fly's wings in a spiderweb. It shook the lives of everyone else in the vicinity, and the resulting vibrations shook other lives, and so on until the whole world was a-tremble with the shock waves of that one single choice. The world, Bijou suddenly saw, was nothing but a web of these interactions. Everything qualified everything else.

She felt lightheaded with the implications, and wondered if this was how a precisian saw the universe.

She had no idea how to explain what she had just comprehended to Salamander, though. So she just said, "You're not alone, my dear. You have us. I'll find a way to prove it to you."

The look Salamander gave her was serious, thoughtful. Bijou felt a warmth in her chest. A sense of sisterhood, she thought suddenly. Belonging. This was what they meant by that.

She had made a friend.

Eleven

WHEN THE SUN set, Bijou went into the desert. By herself, this time, except for a driver who she instructed to wait by the vehicle. Only a fool or a Wizard—or a fool of a Wizard—braved the Mother Desert alone. And having done it once didn't make Bijou eager to try it again.

She wasn't going into Erem this time, but only to the edge of the erg—the shore of the sea of sand.

No one is alone, Bijou told herself for the humor of it as she picked her way across moonlit sand. She carried a spade and a sieve and a bucket. She walked along the ridge of the dune where the sand was firmest, allowing her Wizardly intuition to guide her. She held the spade out before her like a dowsing rod.

The car was a dim shape at the edge of the road behind her. The dunes stretched out under the single moon's silver light, their sunlit colors of caramel and cinnamon faded to charcoal mystery.

The sound of sand grains hissing against each other filled her awareness. The same unrelenting wind that hopped the grains one over another, walking the dunes across the desert like endless stately waves of solid earth, whipped the snakes of her hair forward, slapping her cheeks. She drew a fold of her scarf across her nose and mouth and—rather than shutting the desert out—let it in.

The dune beneath her feet was a virtual mountain of sand. Even now, with sundown hours behind, it radiated heat through the soles of her shoes. Bijou shuffled forward, every step raising the starched-linen scent of hot sand and starting another cascade of sand grains hopping before the wind.

The spade dipped toward earth.

Where it pointed, she crouched down and began to dig. She reached deep with senses honed by over a decade of wizarding, and found all the things that had once been alive, buried in the depths of the dune. One in particular interested her. She let her awareness fill it, tickle it up, call it wriggling through packed sand while she, in turn, dug to meet it. A long-mummified horned viper slept beneath the sand waves of the Mother Desert. Bijou called it forth.

As with the horses and the camel, it was only Bijou's will that animated the snake. She felt the pressure and slip of the sand against its bones. She felt the dead snake's rib-bones grab at that sand and pull it forward, dried sinew crackling. Magic held its bones together now, when no mere withered hide could do so.

Eventually, Bijou saw the bottom of the pit she was digging begin to collapse in on itself and set her spade aside. Her palms were raw from the grit caught between her hands and the spade. Her fingernails bore dark crescents of dirt.

The dead snake hunched itself from the sand and coiled stiffly. Having thrust her spade upright into the earth, Bijou used her hands to assist the viper into the bucket.

Her workshop was separate from the space she shared with Kaulas, as was his. Wizards' workshops were notoriously bad places for eating and sleeping, but for the time being Bijou scarcely left hers. She slept on a pile of cushions in the corner—when she slept—and she took her meals on a tray—although as often as not, she forgot to eat them before the tea was long cold.

First the skeleton must be cleaned, which was a meticulous and painstaking process of scraping away skin and flesh that had hardened to the consistency of old leather. The bones were fragile—terribly delicate, and there were so many of them.

Having cleaned them, Bijou soaked them in a solution that would bleach and strengthen them. While they were resting, she opened shutters and doors to clear the noxious fumes. Then she began work on the armature.

She chose jewels the rust and brown and golden colors of the desert, the colors the snake had worn in its lifetime: tiger eye, citrine, topaz. Jasper and agates. Smoky quartz. Petrified wood. Boulder opal. Normally, she would have left the bones bare to the sight, reinforced with a delicate filigree of metalwork into which the jewels could be set. But in this case, she made it an armature of segmented brass, concealing the bones within its protective shell. It was work with forge and hammer, and with every beat of her mallet against the anvil she thought of Dr. Liebelos hammering the Book into existence, and what they had done to stop her. She sweated over the forge in the relative cool of night, and the heat made her think of Erem. She chased the scaled plates with intricate designs, and set those designs with ten thousand chips of colored mineral. Ambrosias rattled around the laboratory, fetching tools and materials as necessary, without being asked. He knew her methods.

She re-articulated the skeleton with wire, stringing each bone as if constructing a fantastic, architectural necklace. When that was done, she slipped the skeleton into its case and fixed each rib to the metal body with tiny prongs such as one would use to set a stone.

She sealed the two halves along an invisible seam. She set a platinum spring set with pink sapphires in its mouth to act as a tongue, and she lined its upper lip with tiny diamonds to represent the pits such snakes used to detect the warmth of living prey.

Magic wouldn't work without symbolism.

In its empty sockets, where the brass opened gaps to show the bone, she set two lumps of red amber to serve as its eyes. But not before, with her jeweler's tools, she carved the shape of a brain in gray coral and hinged it within.

That was what she was working on when, on the fourth day, Kaulas came to the door in person. Bijou did not speak to him herself. They had an unspoken agreement. They did not bother one another during projects.

Bijou told the *kapikulu* who guarded her door to turn Kaulas away. It was a measure of the courage of *kapikulu* that the man did as she asked, with no blanching or temporizing, even in the face of a necromancer.

She could not turn away Prince Salih, who appeared the next day. It was his house that she lived in—or his father's house, which would eventually be his brother's. Not quite the same thing, perhaps, but much as she itched to be about her work it was a foolish Wizard who alienated her patron.

And this was not, she had to admit, a matter of life and death.

The *kapikulu* admitted him to her laboratory. He looked strangely at home there, standing in his good linen robes on the fire-scarred floor, among acid-stained slate work tables.

She had to let him in and hear him out. But she didn't have to stop her work. Well, all right: protocol would have demanded more courtesy. But Bijou and the prince were friends.

He crossed the room to stand opposite her, watching as she manipulated her delicate tools. You couldn't squeeze a stone brain into an intact cranium, of course—so she'd hinged the snake's skull, and was now making delicate attachments with gold and platinum wire to hold the brain steady within. The flashes of color veining the boulder opal caught light as she angled the stand this way and that. For a few moments, the prince simply stood, hands folded, and watched her.

It wasn't the first time. But she didn't think he'd just dropped by out of curiosity this time.

For the first time, she wondered what it meant to Kaulas that Prince Salih had privileges he did not.

"Bijou," the prince said at last. "Why do you work so feverishly? Nobody's death is at hand."

She squinted through a loupe and twisted two fine wires together. She didn't know how to say what she'd learned, how to express what she was missing. That thing—that human thing—that had always been a mystery to her was now laid bare, and acknowledging it had become a passion, an obsession. Like a fresh grief, it was never far from her thoughts.

Finally, helplessly, she set her hair-fine pliers down. She reached for a soldering iron, the tip smoking-hot, and paused with it raised in her hand.

"If I make something real," she said to the prince. "Something tangible. Then no matter what happens, what was real is real."

"Are you in love with her?" he asked.

The idea had never occurred to her. Her hand was trembling, so she did not touch the wires, even though she knew the iron was growing cold.

"No," she said finally, having examined her emotions. "Not in the way you mean."

"Then what? I've never seen you..." He sighed. "So engaged with anything that was not your work, or a combat, or a contest."

Bijou shrugged. She set the iron to heat once more. She took the loupe out of her eye.

"We have a lot in common," she said.

"Like Kaulas?" His face was calm, placid. She did not know if he'd intended it as a gut-punch, or just a point of information.

"I'm not surprised if he's wooing her," she said at last. "If that's what you're asking."

The prince stroked his beard, a frown pulling long lines into existence around his eyes. "I care about you," he said. "And Kaulas. And I *need* you both."

"No one is alone," Bijou affirmed, pleased that he understood. "Don't worry, my prince. I am ever your right hand."

WHEN THE SNAKE was complete, at last she slept. And then she rose and bathed and dressed, aware that her clothes hung on her loosely. Her hair still swinging damp, she went to where the jeweled serpent hung in its padded rests on the work table.

She laid a hand atop its head, fitted her mouth over the nostrils, and blew a breath of life into its hollow interior.

That was all it took: no incantations and no spells. The intention had been fixed by the work she performed.

The snake-artifice pulled back, suddenly liquidly alive, and slithered to the worktop. There it coiled, slowly orienting itself—to judge by the swing of its head and the flicker of a jeweled tongue.

Bijou coaxed it up her arm and took it to visit her friend.

SALAMANDER SAT BY herself in the shade of the garden, idly picking seeds from a half-pomegranate and tossing them to the birds. A few overlooked bits scattered the tile table before her like a fistful of rubies.

She looked up when Bijou came forward, and smiled. "I had heard you were closeted on some project. I missed you."

"I was," Bijou said. She'd left Ambrosias behind for once. "Doing better?"

"There are good days," Salamander said. The pinch of her lips suggested this might be one of the other sort. "Will you sit?"

"I have a gift for you," Bijou said. She perched on the edge of the stool opposite Salamander and rested the tips of her left fingers on the table top. Warmed by her heat, the artifice's stone and metal skin felt neutral, like her own flesh touching her. It slid down her arm inside the sleeve.

Salamander watched, rapt, as the serpent slipped its head from Bijou's cuff, tasting the air with a sparkling tongue. "Oh, my—"

She looked up at Bijou, eyes wide. "You made that?"

Bijou smiled an answer.

"It's like jewelry," Salamander said. "I can't take that."

"You can and will," Bijou said. "I made it for no one else. You will have to name it—"

If Salamander had been about to argue, Bijou's tone brought her up short. She raised both hands as in surrender.

"All right. I hope it doesn't eat much."

Bijou laughed. The serpent coiled across the table, bridging the distance between them. Its jeweled scales rasped and rattled on the tile, casting a scintilla of reflections from the light dripping through the leaves of the tree they sat beneath.

"Just a clockwork nightingale now and again."

Salamander held her hand out tentatively. The serpent scraped a tonguetip across it, hesitated, then slithered toward her as if its mind had been abruptly made up. As it climbed Salamander's arm to drape around her neck, she said, "It's so heavy!"

"It's stone and metal," Bijou said. "As heavy as the living snake. And a bit cleverer, perhaps. What will you name it?"

"I need to think about it," Salamander said. "It doesn't seem like a decision to be made lightly. Bijou—"

"Ask," Bijou said. "I'm not good at answering, but for you I will try."

"Why?"

That was an easy one. What she wanted to say stuck in her throat, though, as if it were some huge admission of vulnerability. The vulnerability that Bijou had never allowed herself—not since she left her childhood behind.

She swallowed. "You are never alone," Bijou said finally, hoping Salamander would understand.

Maybe she did. Because she just stared for a moment, and then she reached out with the hand not burdened by artifice, and squeezed Bijou's fingers lightly once.